To L. who helped me form a vision of life as it should be.

To Rowan who shared his love of *Don Quixote*.

And to Adam, always.

When life itself seems lunatic, who knows where madness lies? Perhaps to be too practical is madness. To surrender dreams — this may be madness. … — and maddest of all: to see life as it is, and not as it should be.

…

Until death it is all life.

Miguel de Cervantes, *Don Quixote*

Part I

Softly
August 1976

She watches Miriam sleep; olive skin, hair a tangle of soot and pitch. Four years and many defeats ago, Miriam had told her that she'd chosen her for three things: the thick fair plait that swung below her waist; that she was so small; and for her name. Cassie thinks of herself as the ram caught in the thicket, the replacement sacrifice when Abraham was no longer compelled to kill his son. She continually warns Miriam not to go looking for trouble. Let's find another road, she says. But she hadn't seen trouble coming today.

God, this is the end of the story. I can't go on, she says to the night.

Miriam's breath catches and she turns in her sleep. Does Miriam whisper something? Cassie reaches out, strokes Miriam's face, still wet, leans forward, brushes lips against salt dew, too soft to be a kiss, but Miriam's eyes open and she holds out her arms, a shudder of sobs. Cassie presses into the circle of limbs, wishes she could cry.

She sees Miriam on the beach, hurling a rock at the naked man who had her imprisoned in a sticky grasp; hissing — everything will be all right as long as she doesn't struggle.

She remembers feet on white sand, the rub of grains keening above the percussion of waves, Miriam circling away, the sudden halt. Miriam has described the sensations a thousand-thousand times. She will not let Cassie utter the pejorative word, 'fit'. There is a moment of sadness, opaque dark that drops and is gone, torn by the light. Miriam is transfigured: dazzling, serene; the beatific smile an instant before the unbearable moment — the uneven jerk of her limbs, the stare signalling her absence.

Cassie remembers the man grabbing Miriam, how he flinched from the rush of sound, the rising wail marking the boundary between rapture and unconsciousness. How he let Miriam fall, reached out a foot to prod her, as though Miriam might savage him, might be dead. She sees him bending over the crumpled form, pulling at the flimsy summer skirt.

Cassie can't remember whether she had shouted as she ran back, sand squealing under her feet. When did she lift the rock? The story and the facts must match; the ancients didn't start their tales any way they wanted, she tells herself; keep track, you must keep track or it's the end of the story.

I'm your Ben Haddaj, Miriam says through tears. I'm supposed to save you, my enchanted girl.

Cassie nods. She does not see the enchantment, only story and facts aligned. Miriam is Ben Haddaj. She is Casilda. She is not Cassie McManus from the Lawn's Estate. In this lifetime Ben Haddaj will save her and they will be together forever. She clings to Miriam, but cannot weep.

Once there was a Moorish princess, Casilda, daughter of the

king of Toledo and a Berber girl who died in childbirth. She had long golden hair, green eyes, pale skin. She wore only white or the palest blue, almost white, like the halo of sky around the sun.

Cassie's thick plaits are fair, not golden, her eyes grey. These are signs of enchantment, Miriam insists. Cassie sees only the story that Miriam tells; belief is her gift.

Silly Silda, Miriam had said that first day when Cassie dropped the pile of exercise books on the way back to the classroom.

Sorry?

Silda, it's short for your true name — Casilda.

No, Cassie's short for Catherine. It's a family thing, Cassie. Probably someone was short-tongued four generations back, my mam says. Cathy became Cassie. I don't know. There's at least one in every generation: my aunt is Catherine Anne, my nanna, great-gran — all called Cassie.

Miriam shook her head. Catherine Anne McManus is only what you seem to be — it's an enchantment. You are Casilda of the Rising Moon. Have you read the book?

Miriam didn't wait for a response.

I'm not what I seem either. Ben Haddaj at your service. She bowed, her arm flourishing in some courtly gesture borrowed from a film or book. I was the prince your sister, Zoraida, was in love with. I cured you when you were dying, and was promised to your sister to marry, but I was in love with Casilda, and I wanted to stop pretending to be a Muslim prince, wanted to go back to my Jewish roots.

You set your father's prisoners free, went to Castile, became a Christian saint. We lost each other nine centuries ago, but we're destined to meet again and again, perhaps until we resolve our story. Have you heard of metempsychosis?

She hardly waited for Cassie to shake her head before going on:

Transmigration of souls. Gilgul Neshamot in Kabbalah.

Miriam sighed melodramatically. Don't worry, you'll soon understand. We've been numerous people through the ages, some famous like Leonidas and Gorgo in Sparta, some disappeared into history. We've even crossed through time to find each other — in Hungary when you were Selene Solweig Virag. I think we were most truly ourselves as Ben Haddaj and Casilda, but I always recognise you. I knew you as soon as I heard your name. Do you like reading?

Yes, all the time.

But not the right things, I suppose. You need saving, and educating. The family that's enchanted you, what kind of people are they? It doesn't matter. I'm here now.

Sorry?

I recognised you because you're so small and pale. And your hair. She had tugged on Cassie's long plait, laughed. And if you get out of control this is handy for pulling you back.

Cassie had tucked her plait in front and said nothing.

Are you an only child?

I've got a sister, Mandy. She's almost seventeen.

Yes, of course. Casilda must have her sister. Zoraida.

Sorry?

Your sister is really Zoraida. She's always loved you, but she won't understand you. You must take great care. Don't trust her. And a brother?

No, just Mandy. My mam's youngest brother lived with us till he got married. Pat — he was like a brother, sort of ...

Ahmed.

From the same story?

It's not a story, Casilda. It's who you really are — this is just an enchantment. Miriam waved a hand around Cassie, outlining her theatrically. Ahmed will pursue you when you try to become your real self. She sighed. But we will prevail. In this incarnation, I've got four sisters. We're all brilliant, of course, but me most of all. We're Jewish. Do you know what that is?'

Yes, I'm not stupid.

And spirited. I like that.

Cassie imagines telling her family what happened on the beach, but what did happen? The rock hit, but not hard enough. She remembers hands around her throat, rough breath, white cotton tearing, falling onto sand. And then? She remembers a Labrador jumping, barking, a soft Scot's accent like Miriam's father, asking are you all right, what's your name, don't worry, you'll be okay now, hands lifting her; a woman in shorts made of old jeans, soft blue t-shirt, soothing Miriam; two quiet children, a boy of about ten with his mother's round face and doe-alert eyes, the girl a little older, sandy curls, standing back, silent, letting their parents take care of two dishevelled girls on a white beach near Nairn. What could she tell her parents? The parents who had enchanted Casilda and had no idea who she was?

Miriam strokes her hair. Silly Silda, she says, and smiles, you'll be all right. I'm with you now. Cassie nods and Miriam huddles close to her, turns and is asleep in an instant.

Later her dad will nod politely as Mr Jacobs explains that on the beach there was a man, that he had grabbed Miriam, that Cassie had not run away and left her, but ran back, threw a rock, that the man had … Her father will say thank you, that they understand, that these things … Her mum will offer Mr Jacobs a cup of tea, her parents glancing at each other furtively, wondering how they ended up with her, this clever daughter who has always been lost in books or day dreams, who doesn't have the sense to look after herself. Later they will whisper about that Jewish family filling her head with notions: opera, trips, university; all that strange food. And now?

What had happened on the beach? Miriam's soft-spoken father won't look at her. In the night she hears weeping through the flimsy caravan walls. Surely Miriam's mother wouldn't cry for her? But even Judith has been … what? Solicitous? Kind? Cassie is not sure she trusts kindness. A thought of Sean comes to her.

You should take Cassie with you, Mandy had told Sean, the summer before Cassie had started grammar school. She's always been into animals and Mam won't have pets in the house. All she does is read weird books. It can't be good for her.

At the stables the horse loomed over Cassie.

I'll put you on this one, Sean said. She's not as skittish as some and I'll keep you on the rein to start with. We'll just walk you out the first few times.

Cassie stared up at the dark coat, walked towards the head, the eye limpid and enquiring.

She's called Sugar Daddy's Baby, Sean said, laughing. I think Sugar is fine though.

Sugar blew softly, bobbed her head once, twice, rapidly, blew again.

Let her sniff your hand, Sean told her. Good. See how her ears are pointing forward, that's good. Give her neck a scratch.

Cassie reached up, fingering through the hot coat as Sugar nodded.

Three months later, mounted on Sugar, they'd rode out across the fields to Mill Beck, skirted Wardle Wood to come back towards Liverton. You're a natural, Sean pronounced, fantastic. Can't even get Mandy to come and watch.

She says it smells, Cassie called, concentrating on Sugar.

How would she know? She's never been here.

You're too delicate, Cassie. I know the Berber in you loves those Arab horses, but remember you are Casilda, not Zoraida.

By their third year at school, Miriam had begun a campaign against horse riding, though Cassie continued to go to the stable sporadically.

Not next Saturday, Miriam had commanded. I'm singing at a concert in Sedgefield. You can stay with us on Friday night. There's a rehearsal in the afternoon so we have to go early. I'm playing too — Chopin's Prelude in B minor and Mendelsohn's Song Without Words. Tell Sean you can't go riding. And tell him to stop giving you those awful records.

Gordon Lightfoot's okay. I liked the last one he gave me and you liked the one before — *Don Quixote*.

The last one was slush. *Sundown*? And 'Don Quixote' is the only decent track on the eponymous album and only then because it's got literary allusion. Really, Cassie, it's very hard to educate you sometimes. You are still reading the book?

Yes.

And?

It's a bit … I mean I just hope my mother doesn't find it.

Madame Bovary? Good grief, Cassie. Those people are so prudish. Such *am haaretz*. I don't know how you stand it. And Sean is a *schlub*. You must keep reading.

I will.

Good. It's a cautionary tale, Casilda. Never betray anyone, that way terrible consequences lie. Emma is driven mad by living in books, by wanting life to emulate fiction; just like Quixote, just like your sister Zoraida might have been if she hadn't been saved from her romantic swooning by Prince Sancho. But I fear for her in this life. I can't believe Amanda reads those pitiful Mills and Boon books while her boyfriend feeds you musical slop. Romance is not neutral, Cassie, it rots the soul like sugar rots the teeth.

Schlub. The word played in Cassie's head as she stood by the stable door. She remembered thinking how she would have to be driven home by him. The LP was at her feet, *Summertime Dream*. Her fifteenth birthday. Sean had brought the carefully wrapped disc to the stable because she'd be in Scotland with Miriam and her family on her 'big day'. A birthday kiss he'd said. His arms pinning her. Tongue and teeth, scents of brittle hay dust, ammonia, leather, jarring of her thin spine against wood, writhing free, the scratch scoured down his left cheek as she flailed away, the names that called after her. She'd walked towards the car, eyes down, half closed, huddled into the seat, said nothing.

Miriam sleeps. Cassie tries to remember the beach. The story and the facts must match. Hands around her throat, rough breath, white cotton tearing, falling onto sand …

She listens to Miriam's soft breathing, strokes the silk dark hair that bobs around her neck. God, is this the end of the story? Can I go on? She asks the night.

June–July 1977

The unreason of the world is more insane than any fiction.

High summer and the Queen lights beacons at Windsor Castle. The signal for national celebrations of her Silver Jubilee. Not festive misrule, of course, but only ritual pretence; not masquerade or metamorphosis, but burning to preserve what is.

June 7 and crowds line the streets as Her Majesty, Queen Elizabeth II, processes to St Paul's Cathedral. A service of thanksgiving attended by world leaders: James Callaghan PM; Jimmy Carter, President, so many past prime ministers. Afterwards, a civilised luncheon at the Guildhall, procession to the palace, a million people lining the streets; around the Commonwealth 500 million watching on TV. Across the nation, towns and villages festooned with bunting, street parties celebrating this 'united kingdom'.

I wish to inform you that I shall personally attend the meeting and also be present at all the functions organised for the celebrations of the Silver Jubilee of her Majesty the Queen, Idi Amin had written, but on the day he fails to come to London with a delegation of dancers of the heartbeat of Africa.

Instead, Malcolm MacLaren and the Sex Pistols are arrested, attempting to sail the Thames singing their version of 'God Save the Queen'.

A month later, Maureen Long, 42, is attacked. It is thought that her assailant is the Yorkshire Ripper; *Gay News* is found guilty of blasphemous libel; the case brought by Mary Whitehouse's National Viewers and Listeners Association; Denis Healey announces an attack on inflation with a phased return to free collective bargaining and Energy Secretary, Tony Benn, announces that Drax B power station will go ahead at a cost of £600 million.

The unreason of the world is more insane than any fiction.

And now for the weather: After a rainy start, July is expected to become warm and sunny, though north-easterly wind will bring cool spells in the second week and the second half of the month is expected to be cooler.

Does Your Mother Know?
July 1977

Miriam leads Cassie across a small dirt track running diagonally off the road. In the autumn the field below Eston hills will be full of bramble pickers, fathers with small children, but today the fruits are small and green, the thorns vicious. They negotiate the steeply rising track, crowded on either side by tall ferns and alders. Fat blue bottles buzz around them.

We'll make for Draco's Rock, Miriam says.

How long ago was it that Miriam had persuaded Cassie to cycle here before dawn? They had intended to climb to the rock slab butting against the final rise of the hills. If they saw the sun rise over the peak then the slab would move aside for them.

The episode had taken Miriam before they reached Kirkleatham. Cassie squatted against the church wall, cold, shaking, the morning still dark. She watched the tremor begin in Miriam's right arm, the strange smile, the low moan that became a steady note, intoned, the unnatural absence creeping across her face as unconsciousness took her. She had run to the little row of cottages behind the church and beaten on the first door until someone came.

Judith was incandescent. That scrawny girl who picked at her food, dropped her 'h's, lived on that estate; scum scraped from the slums of Southbank to be deposited in herds in tacky council houses; paper-thin walls, the smell of chip-fat and vinegar, smoke-stains, drives blocked with scrap cars.

We will never have another chance to enter the other world, Miriam had told her. Not while you are under this present enchantment, Casilda.

Today they climb to the top.

Casilda's warring father Alamun, a dark and dangerous Moor, filled his dungeons with Christian knights, captured in battle by his son, Ahmed.

Miriam pauses to stroke Cassie's hair, which she has commanded her to leave loose.

Casilda was unlike her family, especially her half sister, Zoraida, wild, dark, driven stupid by reading romances. Ahmed decided Zoraida should marry Ben Haddaj, everything Zoraida wanted, except that he didn't love her. At night he would hide in the shadows to glimpse Casilda and so learnt her secret: that she took food to the prisoners in the dungeons, learnt their stories, gave her pure heart to God.

Cassie smiles and nods, continues up the incline ahead.

Zoraida founded a great dynasty with a prince of Northern Spain. And Ben Haddaj? Knowing that I could never be with you in that life, my darling Casilda, I turned to the religion of my ancestors, died making my way to Israel to find my spiritual roots.

Miriam exhales, clutches both hands together in the air.

But we live on, born generation after generation until we are finally united.

Cassie sees Ben Haddaj before her, smiles. The story and the facts are one. Belief is her gift.

Tanasukh, she says.

Miriam smiles. Yes, the Islamic version of transmigration of souls, but heretical for them. Though not for less Orthodox Sufis, who are always an interesting group and know about bunuz too — how one soul can project into another, not just pass down generations.

Miriam glances ahead towards the path, where it becomes steeper, makes a grab for Cassie.

Get down, Casilda.

She pulls Cassie into a clump of ferns, crouches with her as an elderly couple pass, a fat black mongrel panting behind them.

Moorish scouts sent to re-capture you. Ahmed will never rest until he returns you to Toledo. He has spies everywhere and hates me for rejecting Zoraida. If he found us together there's no saying what cruelties he'd be capable of.

Miriam half stands, peers at the backs of the retreating couple.

He's hunting with hounds, but we are safe for the moment. We must move quickly. Keep to the side of the track.

Miriam darts from the ferns, Cassie following.

At Draco's Rock they spread cardigans on the dusty ground, sit to share Judith's picnic, moist chicken, homemade fruit jam in homemade bread, doughy cookies. The lemonade is cold in the flask, grains of flesh floating in tart liquid.

Christopher Walters has a thing for you, Miriam announces. You do realise?

No.

He asked if you'd be at Joanne's party.

But you don't want to go.

I don't want any scenes. Would you go out with him? Judith thinks we should have boyfriends. She thinks you're holding me back. Perhaps you want a boyfriend.

Miriam stands, her back to the rock, face flushed.

Don't Miriam. There's nothing to get upset over.

I'm just asking what you want. I'm the one who has guarded our connection across centuries. Maybe you'd prefer to be with Christopher Walters.

No.

Cassie holds out a hand and Miriam squats next to her, takes Cassie's face in her palms, leans her head on Cassie's shoulder, begins to cry.

We should be getting back. Miriam is brisk again. I'll go ahead. We have to be careful. We've travelled through nine centuries to be together. No doubt our persecutors will do the same. I suspect Christopher Walters is one of Ahmed's men. Vigilance, Casilda.

Miriam pulls Cassie to her feet, kisses her lightly.

My mother knows everything, she whispers.

Cassie shifts uneasily, thinks back to earlier that day, Miriam waving the new record, *I Pagliacci*.

Judith has tickets for York festival. We're going to hear the *1812* in the park with canons firing over the lake. Daddy will drive us. We can stay with Rebecca and Sam overnight. Won't that be fun?

Cassie had agreed, trying not to think of how much Miriam's oldest sister disliked her, but wishing it was any of Miriam's other sisters who lived in York, Hannah or Deborah, or preferably Sarah, who had recently finished her degree in Drama at Lancaster, wore fab hippie clothes and had an enviable way of calming Miriam.

Miriam stood in front of her full-length mirror mouthing the words of the record, gesturing theatrically. She turned to the bed where Cassie crouched, hugging her knees.

I expect you will break my heart one day.

Cassie opened her mouth, but said nothing.

Miriam dived onto the bed, arranged herself: an effigy on a sarcophagus.

I can see myself dying for love in this life as in previous lives.

In the slip between worlds Cassie had blurted laughter; for a moment she was Cassie McManus, sixteen, thin, pretty, with a party invite that tempted her more than the *1812* in York Museum Gardens. But don't bring Miriam, Joanne had said, slipping a party invitation into her coat pocket in the cloakroom.

Miriam rolled over, tugged hard on her hair. You deserved that, you heartless hussy; laughing at my distress, plotting your betrayal.

Cassie pulled herself closer in, silent.

There, there. You know I always forgive you. You saved me on the beach, remember. My fragile girl rescuing her knight.

When Judith walked in, Miriam was leaning against Cassie, stroking her hair, kissing the corner of her mouth.

Judith had looked away, began to bustle with clothes cast aside on the floor, fussed with the curtains. You two girls should be out getting fresh air before this weather breaks, she said, still turned away from them. You should make the most of what little summer we get. And you have that party tonight. You should walk into town and get a card for the girl whose birthday it is.

We're not going.

Judith said nothing, turned back towards them, pursing her lips

Cassie doesn't want to go.

Judith rolled her eyes. You two spend too much time huddled away. You should be out with friends. Wouldn't you enjoy a party, Cassie?

Cassie shrugged.

Well at least go for a walk. You've got all day.

Miriam pulled a face.

Really, Miriam. Come on, turn that music off and get yourselves outside. All this … this mooning around … it's not … you need fresh air and …

Judith picked up the oddments of clothing she'd put down on a chair, straightening the cushions.

It might be cooler at the beach, Cassie ventured.

Miriam made a whining noise. The beach will be full of Penny Dean clones. If I'm going to be forced out of my home then it will have to be the hills. At least we can look down on *hoi polloi* from there.

Good, I'll make you some sandwiches. Cassie, you can manage a flask of lemonade in your duffle bag, can't you? Judith turned. You'll keep an eye on her, Cassie?

Yes, Mrs Jacobs.

Maybe Cassie is right, Miriam. There are more people around at the beach. I don't want you having an attack and …

I'm fine, Mother. There'll be picnickers and all sorts on the beach today. Unbearable.

Judith paused, opened her mouth, left them alone.

Miriam smiles at Cassie. Silly, Silda. Didn't you realise she's always known? She kisses Cassie again, brushing the corner of her mouth. She rests her hands on Cassie's shoulders. My mother's known everything since I met you.

At eleven? But …

She knew how it would go. Once she was Sulema, you know.

Judith?

Yes. I know she doesn't seem as though she's devoted to you in this life, but she's become confused over the years. In her own way everything she does is for you, Casilda. She was your nursemaid, your confidante, your shadow. She made the pilgrimage with you to Castile, saw you perform miracles, saw your saintliness. She knew I loved you, as Ben Haddaj, but knew I was promised to your sister, Zoraida, and that I never returned from my pilgrimage to marry her. She didn't realise that I was drowned. Only Ahmed discovered what had happened to Ben Haddaj, Prince of Zaragoza. He found out much later when he made his own pilgrimage to Mecca and became a holy man himself. Sulema simply wants you to fulfil your destiny as Saint Casilda.

But she's Jewish …

Judith is Jewish, as I was as Ben Haddaj, at least at the end, but as Sulema she was your Muslim nursemaid, and, later, your Christian servant. She's protecting you, my Silly Silda, from me. Remember after the first year at school, how she tried to have us put in different classes?

Cassie nods.

All that stuff about you being a bad influence, from a bad family, that's just the cover story, my sweetness. It's me who she thinks will lead you astray, not the other way round.

Cassie nods again. For five years she has seen only the story that Miriam tells. Belief is her gift.

My mother knows everything, Miriam whispers again. She turns to descend the hill, freezes. Penny Dean, she hisses, quick. Miriam pulls at Cassie to crouch.

Miriam!

Shhh. I'm fine.

I thought you were having … Cassie looks for the tremor, there is nothing, but Miriam pales.

Do you smell that? Woodsmoke and something else — like camphor and lemon, sage on the mountainside. We're in danger, Cassie. Ancient Greece, I think. Yes — look.

Cassie obediently peers over the boulder sheltering them from being seen by Penny Dean and a group of girls from school, making their way up the path she and Miriam recently descended.

Persian scouts. Oh … I'm chanelling Leonidas. You must channel Gorgo, quick, quick, Cassie.

Miriam crouches, head in her hands. Gorgo?

Yes.

Keep still, Gorgo. Let them pass. And silence.

Cassie crouches, watching Miriam for signs of tremor. A bead of sweat snakes down Miriam's face, she is paler with each second. They listen to the girls pass beyond the boulder, Penny's shrill voice entertaining the rest. Up here, Penny calls, and Miriam lets out a long breath.

It's worse than I thought, Gorgo, Miriam says when the

group are out of earshot. Not mere scouts. That one is Ephialtes, who will betray our secret paths to the enemy, cause my death and the deaths of all those loyal to Greece, all but the cowardly Thebans, who will surrender to Xerxes rather than die with honour. I have only a few days left to the end now. You must stay strong, my Queen, continue to counsel our son as you have me, as you did your father, my half-brother, Cleomenes. Remember your wisdom, only Spartan women can rule men because only Spartan women give birth to men. When I'm gone, marry a good man and have good children. We will never give up our arms, Gorgo. They must come and take them.

Yes, Cassie assents. She looks at the distant figures, sees not Penny and her friends but everything as Miriam describes. The heat haze on the dusty path, the scent of sage, spies marching accompanied by Ephialtes, showing them the way to kill her beloved Leonidas, his three hundred men, the seven hundred loyal Thespians, the nine hundred Helots remaining with her husband, king, general, hero.

Miriam stands, clambers onto the boulder. Come take us if you dare, she shouts after the figures.

Cassie sees the shudder of Miriam's right arm from behind. She misses her footing as she leaps towards the boulder, scraping her shin painfully down the raw rock as Miriam tumbles down the other side, piercing the day with her unnerving wail, a single note. Cassie vaults the stone the second time, is at Miriam's side.

Miriam opens her eyes slowly, looks at Cassie intently, as though trying to remember the name of someone she met once, a long time ago, blinks and focuses, recognition flooding in.

Unbearable, Miriam whispers, but worth it for that moment of ecstasy. I felt heaven descended to earth and swallow me.

I attained God and was saturated with him. You healthy people have no idea what happiness is.

Dostoevsky? Cassie asks. But did you hurt yourself? You fell. Cassie can feel sticky blood trailing her own shin, but ignores it.

My arm, Miriam says. And my head hurts, but of course it will hurt like this all week now, not from the fall. I feel heavy. I can hear the angels whispering in the ether. Soft and sweet.

Cassie nods, feels the length of Miriam's arm. There's a bruise blossoming beneath her shoulder, another on her left shin.

Don't tell Judith, Miriam commands, don't tell my mother. She doesn't have to know everything.

August 1977

The unreason of the world is more insane than any fiction.

Under tight security, the Queen visits Northern Ireland – part of the celebrations of the Silver Jubilee.

Boycott scores his 100th century for England against Australia at Headingley. It's the silly season, not festive misrule or international news. Donna Summer remains at No.1 with 'I Feel Love'.

And now for the weather: Although August temperatures are expected to be lower than average, with higher rainfall, the north will see the best weather, with a sunny month.

Go My Way
August 1977

Silly Silda, didn't I tell you you'd do better than me? Cassie picks up the small post card on the table in the parquet-floored entrance to Saltscar Comprehensive. Langbaurgh High School, Miriam still insists, two years after the grammar school has merged into the new comprehensive. She glances down at the list of O level results, each marked 'A'.

It's the way of it, sweetheart, the protégée outdoing the mentor. But look, I got an A in both Englishes, so I'll forgive you. I'm going to miss this place. You?

Of course.

Do you remember the first day?

Miriam has asked this so many times over the last five years. Cassie nods.

Casilda lived in the Alcazar of Toledo, a mirror of the mother she had never known, the green-eyed Berber girl more than thirty years younger than her husband, Alamun, who had lost his wife within a year, but worshipped the child she left him; Casilda, green-eyed and golden haired, delicate as the rising moon, who pitied the prisoners her brother Ahmed brought home from battle, dreamed the future, and would become a great saint. It was a time of knights and saints, mystics and heroes, magicians and princes. Casilda, born into riches and portrayed in rich silks in the art of Toledo, the darling of her father, left wealth behind to live in a simple cave. She embraced Christianity, lived in simplicity and performed many miracles of healing. Casilda was loved by a Muslim prince, Ismael Ben Haddaj, who returned to the religion of his ancestors, Judaism; a saint who embraces the three great religions of the Western world, and teaches us that compassion crosses all boundaries.

Thank you, Miriam, Miss Baker said, forcing a smile. That was … very instructive.

Oh, there's more. Miriam returned Miss Baker's frozen smile, continued — Casilda was a frail child. When she reached her teens she became more and more ill, an unnatural flow of blood, it's thought. Ben Haddaj cured her once, but when he left to go on a pilgrimage the haemorrhage returned —

Sick cow, Penny Dean whispered to Sally Lewis.

Miriam smiled wider — Casilda refused to allow the Muslim doctors to see or treat her, but begged her father to negotiate safe passage for her to travel to a healing well in Northern Spain. He freed all his Christian prisoners in return for her safety and she was healed at the well of St Vincent, where she went on to live as an anchorite until she was over a hundred.

Miss Baker spoke before Miriam could continue further. That's very interesting, Miriam. Thank you again. And who is leading the class assembly next week? Gillian, I think you're next?

Yes, miss.

Cassie glanced at the bored faces of twenty-two girls.

Who speaks like that? Penny Dean whispered to Sally Lewis, not quite quietly enough. She's such a phoney.

Putz, Miriam hissed as she sat down behind Penny.

Cassie shook her head. If only Miriam would avoid trouble.

So can she really do it?

What?

Mad Miriam. Can she really get in touch with dead people? All that, what does she call it? Free writing? It's a bit weird isn't it?

You should ask her yourself, Cassie replied.

Yeah, I did. She told me she doesn't talk to *hoi polloi*. It's just that my sister died. I thought …

Oh, Marcia, I didn't know. I mean …

No, it was ages ago. I don't really remember her. I just thought …

I'm not sure. I mean it might be … sort of upsetting … I don't know if it would be a good idea …

No, maybe not. But that free writing thing is weird. It got me thinking …

It's called automatic writing. Psychography.

Yeah? I saw her doing it yesterday. She looked really out of it, but she's not in school today.

She had an attack.

Someone attacked her cos of the writing?

No. Epilepsy. Penny and Sally snuck up while she was — she goes somewhere else … when she's in that … that trance … she gets these other people and …

Gets them?

Channels them. It's like someone else coming through her body. Penny screeched in her ear and it … I don't know exactly what happened. I was in the library. I think the shock …

Yeah, and how many times a week does Miss Baker tell us never to upset Miriam? Bet Penny and Sally are for it. And Miriam's mother will be putting in a word with Miss Doone, no doubt. Wouldn't want to cross Miriam's mother, eh?

Come on Miriam, show us what you can do. If it's true, you'd show us.

Miriam glowered, dark eyes narrowed.

Just ignore them. Miriam, Cassie begged.

Aw come on, Cassie. Let her show us.

Jew-bitch, someone hissed from the growing crowd behind Cassie. She turned, pale skin flaring pink, ready to defend, but behind her every girl smiled sweetly.

We just want to see, Marcia said mildly, smiling at Cassie.

If a lion could speak, we could not understand him, Miriam said to the girls massing around her.

Eh? You on something or what? Penny Dean asked, beginning to laugh as though she'd told the funniest joke.

Just let her talk, Marcia said.

Yes, added Joanne Leigh, pushing forward so that the crowd parted slightly for the tall thirteen year old, voted class president the day before. We're interested, Miriam. Joanne pushed back springy red hair, leaned slightly as she talked. It's fascinating. Is it like a trance? I mean, do people really take you over? Dead people?

It's more complicated, Miriam said.

Across the crowd, Cassie shook her head, mouthed 'no'. Please Miriam, tell them you've got a headache, tell them you feel an attack coming on. Don't go looking for trouble, Miriam. Let's find another road. She hoped Miriam would hear the plea in her head.

I get people from the past. Some of them are myself, my past lives. I'm not like you, I'm immortal. This is just a mask.

Penny Dean made a farting noise with her mouth and Joanne shot her a disapproving look.

Psychography is metaphysical, it's …

Come again in English, Penny persisted, laughter like gulls braying.

What do you mean, Miriam? If you could …

Yes, as I expected, we're back to Wittgenstein's lion, aren't we?

Penny made a sign to Sally Lewis, circling her index finger around the side of her head: 'lunatic'.

Try to keep it simple, Joanne said, smiling.

Miriam sighed deeply, closed black-brown eyes slowly, moved her head, bell of dark hair shimmering. Give me a piece of paper. Large. And a sharp pencil, not too sharp, so it doesn't break while I'm in flow.

Tools were produced. Miriam sat at a desk, *Sally4Macco* scored into an ink heart at its centre, the throng of girls moving closer.

Not too close, Miriam warned. I need absolute silence. Anyone who doesn't believe should leave now. I will be in a delicate state, the slightest negative vibe could have terrible consequences.

Several girls glanced at Penny.

Don't look at me. I'll believe if I see for myself.

I think she should leave, Miriam said.

No way.

I think you should, Penny, just this time, Joanne reasoned.

She's blinking bonkers, Penny spat back, flouncing from the room, heavy door slamming the silence.

This is a very confused story, Cassie. Marcia's usually such a sensible girl. She's very distressed. Miriam's father had to come from work to collect her and Mrs Jacobs says that there are pills missing. Miss Baker glanced at a piece of paper. Klonapin? You wouldn't know …? It's just that someone mentioned that perhaps … that Miriam might share the …

No. She doesn't.

You're very close. The silence stretched across the afternoon shadow, congealed. Mrs Jacobs thinks … perhaps … maybe you and Miriam … but I've always thought you looked after her, Cassie.

Yes.

This can't happen again. These … sessions … If we can rely on you …

Yes.

Well … I think … perhaps … Maybe you'd best sit in the library till break. I expect Mademoiselle Gillard would prefer not to be interrupted.

Yes.

Thank you, Cassie.

Did you know they didn't used to let them get married? Penny addressed Sally as the two strolled past Miriam threading a daisy chain, hunched on the new-mown grass, green summer scent over sulphur salt-tang air.

Jews couldn't marry? Sally asked, voice raised to match Penny's shrill.

Ha! Should be those as well. No, weirdos — epileptics. They strolled on, out of earshot.

Don't, Cassie said quietly as Miriam had stood, strode after

Penny and Sally. Miriam, don't.

Eugenics, Miriam called loudly, as she held Penny by the elbow briefly. You're a fan are you?

Get lost. Penny jerked her arm away. And don't touch me. Don't ever touch me, you weirdo. It's not like you'll ever get married anyway — one less freaky Jew throwing fits. Miriam Jacobs — end of the line. Drop dead, McManus, Penny added as Cassie scuttled to Miriam's side.

Cassie had watched Penny and Sally stride up the long school field, past the rounders game cheerfully led by Joanne, wild red hair, long limbs running.

Shiksa! Miriam called after the retreating pair. *Farkakt shiksa!*

Miriam, don't.

It's not like they understand.

That's a terrible word.

Shiksa? Miriam laughed, looped the daisy chain around Cassie, once, twice. Moonflowers for Casilda of the rising moon.

The other word, Cassie said. You know what I mean. It doesn't matter what they understand, it demeans you.

Oh, my pure Casilda. Tell me a story. Now.

It's outrageous, Miriam had said, meeting Cassie in the parquet-floored hallway. Everything's spoilt.

They won't be in class with us, Cassie soothed, only in tutor group. We'll only see them at registration and class meetings.

It's not the point. Everything will change, Cassie. And that uniform. What are you thinking?

Cassie looked down at the grey pleated skirt, the pale pink gingham blouse under the grey cardigan. It's not too bad, really.

Miriam snorted. You won't get me wearing it. She stood resolute in navy skirt, pale blue shirt, school tie, navy wool blazer. I didn't pass my eleven-plus to go to Saltscar Comprehensive. This will always be Langbaurgh High School as far as I'm concerned.

Digging the uniform, Cassie, Penny Dean remarked as she walked past them. Can't say the same for mad Miriam there. Can't you do anything with her? Penny laughed at herself and wandered towards the cloakroom.

She'll be pregnant before she takes her O levels, Miriam predicted. With all these boys all over the place, she's bound to be — her and Sally Lewis. Empty headed and no morals.

Don't start looking for trouble, Miriam, term hasn't even begun yet. And we've got our first Latin lesson today.

Miriam smiled. Yes, that's cheering. I suppose we'd better find the form room.

In the classroom familiar girls milled amongst new faces, half a tutor group from the secondary school next door, a mixed group of girls and boys in grey uniforms, only Miriam wore the uniform of one of the former schools making the merger, a concession meant for families who might not be able to afford a new uniform immediately. Miriam chose a double desk in front of Joanne Leigh and her friend, Jane Bingham, a mousy, studious girl who the popular Joanne had known since infant school.

Oh no, Miriam said loudly as two boys took the desk in front of them. We'd better move.

Hi, said one of the boys, before Miriam could gather her things.

Cassie pulled Miriam back towards her seat as she half rose, shook her head almost imperceptibly. Hi.

I'm Christopher. Christopher Walters, said the boy, thick set and high coloured, his mousy hair spiky. And this is Liam Brennan.

A dark-haired boy, long-limbed, turned and grinned. Cassie, isn't it?

Miriam shot a disapproving look.

Yes, I'm sorry, I …

My cousin is going out with your sister. We met at the stables once when you were with Sean.

Ah. Cassie smiled, ignoring the glacial stares and small huffing noises coming from Miriam. Yes, I'm Cassie McManus and this is Miriam Jacobs.

Hi Miriam, both boys said.

Excuse me, Miriam got up from her seat, watching Cassie as she walked towards the door of the classroom. Liam raised an eyebrow.

She okay? Christopher asked.

She doesn't like change, Cassie faltered. I should maybe see how she is.

High strung as a filly I'd say, Liam said, but pretty. He leant his head to one side and watched Miriam as she moved to the back of the classroom.

Forget about it, Li. Penny Dean was at Liam's side. She leant over his desk and flicked a long strand of hair over her shoulder. Mad Miriam doesn't do boys, if you know what I mean.

Yeah? Christopher looked around at Miriam, more interested for a moment, glanced back at Cassie. But you're not … you know …

Cassie watched Miriam hover by the door, checking whether Cassie had followed. Take no notice of Penny, she said to the boys, getting up, noticing Miriam's arm shiver slightly. Oh no, not now, Miriam, not now, she willed.

I'll get help, she heard Joanne say as they ran the short length of the classroom. The assembled teenagers stopped, silenced by the wail emitted as Miriam's face clouded, blank, and she crumpled.

No Miriam today?

She says she's not coming back till the head of year apologises to us all, Cassie told Christopher.

She shouldn't upset herself over the likes of Gazza. He's been caned more times than she's had hot dinners.

Not in front of the whole year, surely?

No, that was a new one. Mr Runcie outdid himself, I'd say. Definitely a sadist that one.

But Gaz would have had the police on him otherwise, Liam put in.

Maybe that's better, Cassie said. He did beat up Sally Lewis.

Yeah, cock-tease ... Sorry. Christopher coloured. I mean she's kind of ... you know. Anyway, I'm not saying he should have hit her, just ...

You think a criminal record is better than being caned? Liam asked, interested.

It's not the middle ages, public beatings, implicating all of us. I've booked a tutorial with Mr Runcie at the end of lunch and that's what I'll be telling him. If a crime has been committed then it's a matter of justice, not vigilante retribution. He has no right to include me in his sordid punishments, or anyone else. It's abusive.

Wow. You're going to say that to Runcie?

Shit! Don't do it, Christopher added. Gazza's really not worth it.

It's not just for that boy; it's for all of us, our humanity. Cassie paused, flushed, aware that she wouldn't have made the speech with Miriam present.

Liam chuckled. Yeah, but here's the thing — you're going to march in there and tell him this on everyone's behalf all by yourself.

Miriam would too if she was here.

But you're not the same as her.

Cassie considered, awkwardness wriggling between pause and thought. I'm not … I mean … I just think he has to know how some of us feel …

Liam raised an eyebrow.

Okay, how I feel.

Well, you might have someone to go into battle with you after all.

Cassie turned to see Miriam in the open doorway of the form room. Her hair, which had grown long over the last year, had been cut into a sleek bob, black tulip petals caressing her shoulders. She'd grown taller than Cassie, who remained shorter than anyone in their year, and had lost the stocky solidity of the previous summer. Miriam smiled, twirled, walked forward.

Judith's handiwork, she said, letting her hand rest lightly on Cassie's arm for a moment.

I thought you weren't …

My parents are with Mr Runcie. We'll have an apology to the year group before the end of the day. You'll see.

Cassie's going to read him the riot act, Christopher put in.

Yeah, dead brave, she is, Liam added.

That won't be necessary, Miriam said, turning her back on the two boys. Let's walk on the field. She took Cassie's arm, led her away.

Outside, Miriam stopped, faced Cassie. My darling Casilda,

she said, you must remember who you are. I know how you feel for wretches, the delicate princess bravely taking bread to the prisoners in your father's dungeons. So compassionate, so oblivious to the dangers to yourself. But you must take care, my Casilda. You're not made for battle, my sweetness.

But …

Miriam held a warning finger over Cassie's mouth.

And those boys. You have to stop encouraging them. She held up her finger again, sighed deeply. I know. I know you don't realise, you're so naïve, Cassie. But I'm here now. I'll always be here.

You Miriam? Gazza stood in front of Miriam and Cassie's desk, thick-necked, shoulders hunched, brown eyes, lip curling under a nose that seemed always to smell something putrid. Well?

I'm Miriam Jacobs.

Yeah? Gazza's lips curled into what might be a smile. You the one that went to Runcie for me? Made him apologise?

Cassie was about to say that it was Miriam's parents, that the apology was for what the year group had been exposed to, not for what was done to the boy who had burst Sally Lewis's lip, blacked her eye, bruised her arms. The story and the facts must match; the ancients didn't tell tales any way they wanted, she thought. But by the door she saw Penny Dean, a group of acolytes around her, sniggering, watching.

Miriam, Cassie whispered, inclining her head towards the door. Miriam.

Push off, Titch, Gazza snapped at her.

Cassie stood but didn't move away.

You got a death wish? Gazza asked, pushing her slightly.

Eh, Gazza, keep your filthy paws to yourself, man. Christopher moved to stand behind Cassie.

Whatever. It's this one I'm interested in. Heard you got the hots for me, Jew-girl. Well, I'm not prejudiced. Meet you later, eh? Near Pacitto's on the front? Make your day, eh? Then you can buy me an ice cream.

By the door, Penny Dean wolf whistled, the group of girls fell around in pantomime laughter. Miriam's face flared, splotches of bitter red, tears filming her eyes. She looked around for an escape, the girls still filling the doorway, burst into noisy tears, began to scream.

Cassie and Miriam lay on the school playing field. The thrum of a mower across the road on the executive housing estate, where Joanne Leigh and Penny Dean lived next door to one another in states of desirable residences.

All done, Miriam said, turning onto her stomach, winding another daisy chain around Cassie.

Cassie smiled.

Ha! Bet you'll get an A in everything anyway.

Perhaps, Cassie consented. Still, good to finish with English and wonderful to have no more exams.

Till the next lot. Miriam sat up, dark eyes sparkling. Are you sure I can't persuade you to take French for A level? *Madame Bovary* in its original language?

Cassie shook her head. I can't give up RE, Miriam. I want to do theology at university.

Miriam sighed. I suppose a saint has to have her religious knowledge.

We'll be together for English and history, Cassie soothed.

And after A levels?

I don't know, Miriam.

You'll go to Oxford or Cambridge.

I don't know. I'm not sure a McManus can do that.

Nonsense. You'll become a great theologian, a mystic, Casilda. Don't forget, maddest of all is to see life as it is, not as it should be.

Cassie rolled over, squashing a line of carefully threaded daisies that had trailed her body.

Oh, Cassie, Miriam's exasperation was a light mockery, but her gaze shifted towards a noise further down the field. Oh, no, those people!

A crowd was forming around two boys, Gary Patterson, Gazza, and a smaller boy, his hair so fair it was almost white, a taut length of wire tensing to hit or leap. The chant of *fight, fight* drifted on the slight summer breeze.

Look at them, a pack of wild beasts, but I will quiet the howling fiends, bring them to order. I must go into battle, my Casilda of the rising moon. This is a just war; there is nothing more worthwhile to God than to wipe out the evildoers.

Miriam, you can't. They're not beasts, they're boys and Gary is … he's violent … you'll get hurt.

No, they are beasts, Casilda. Look carefully, see: rutting animals. Surely by now, Casilda, you must know more about adventure.

Miriam stood, began to run towards the massing throng of chanting teenagers, dodged under the arm of a tall, mousy-haired boy, pushed past Christopher Walters, who took a step back, mouth open, stepped into the centre of the circle and pushed between the boys squaring up to one another.

What the fuck? Cassie heard Gazza say as she edged through the mob. What the fuck are you on, bitch? Fuck off out of here.

The knight's only responsibility is to succour the afflicted, Mr Patterson. I see only the suffering of this unfortunate boy, whatever his misdeeds.

Someone in the herd began to giggle uncontrollably. Gazza swung round, punched the laughing boy hard so that he toppled into the one behind, a melee of cries of pain, fists and feet rolling around one side of the pack as Gazza shifted his gaze back to Miriam, reached one hand around her throat and shook.

Cassie halted, prickled with sweat, watched the tell-tale quiver of Miriam's right arm, the flash of surprise on Gazza's face as the monotone keen filled the air the instant that Christopher and Liam pushed forward, floored Gazza, held him pinned. Miriam fell, face colourless, vacant. Across the field a whistle sounded, over and over, Mr Runcie and two other members of staff racing towards the dispersing flock.

And Miriam, blinking up at Cassie as she knelt by her, struggling to focus, a thin dribble of vomit leaking from the side of her mouth, weak smile, saying, Until death, it's all life, Cassie. Remember.

Ah well, away we must go, Miriam says, pulling Cassie back to the present. And I have a surprise for you. We're going on a walking holiday in the Lake District.

We are? When?

Next week.

But we have college starting …

Not until the week after that.

Judith is going to let us go walking round the Lake District? Just us?

Sarah's just moved there. She has some awful Drama residency with 'underprivileged' children over the summer before she starts teaching at The Lakes School next month. We can stay with her, get busses to walks, and she'll pick us up in the evenings. We've even booked youth hostels so we can do Ambleside and Hawkshead. We've got bikes we can use too, Sarah's and a friend of hers who's lent one.

Cassie smiles, relieved that it is Sarah, of all Miriam's sisters, who will be on hand.

Maybe not the bikes, though, she ventures. My sense of balance is terrible. I'd wobble off the thing if a bus went past or a lorry.

You'll be fine. Miriam waves away the worry.

The first two days of walking go well, short trips from Sarah's tiny cottage. They climb, but not too high, looking down on exquisite lakes while eating sandwiches Sarah has made for them. Cassie sits and writes fragments of poetry while Miriam sprawls on the picnic blanket finding shapes in wispy clouds.

The third day they are booked into the Hawkshead youth hostel. A friend of Sarah's loads their bikes into a van and takes them part of the way. When they've waved David away, they set off on quiet roads, light packs with sandwiches, a flask, thin sleeping-bag liners to use inside the hostel-provided bags.

You're doing fine, Miriam calls periodically as they pedal hard, finding their way through unfamiliar gears.

Cassie relaxes, savours the feel of sun and breeze on her arms.

Watch out! Miriam shouts, jerking Cassie from her reverie. Dragon at the rear, Cassie! Hold steady!

Cassie peers round at the tourist coach and grips the handlebars, concentrates on looking ahead, staying straight, not too close to the edge with its deeply-brambled ditch.

The coach moves out, glides past, catches up with Miriam in front, passes her by.

Cassie breathes out.

Later, at the hostel overlooking Esthwaite Water, they are shown into a dormitory by a boy a little older themselves.

Toby, he says, holding out a hand. My dad's the warden here

and I help out in the summer.

Tobit or Tobias? Miriam asks.

Toby frowns. Tobias, but don't tell anyone. His expression changes to a grin. Just down here, he says, and the girls' bathroom is just opposite.

Thank you, Cassie says.

You look like my girlfriend, Toby offers, as Miriam walks past him into the dormitory. Really like.

Miriam smiles.

By dinner-time there are three other girls in the dormitory. By the time they have eaten dinner, Miriam has offended two of them. Cassie grimaces at her and shakes her head, but knows Miriam will ignore her.

I'm sorry, Casilda, she says, when the girls have left the dorm to play board games in the sitting room for the evening. You know I can't tolerate idiots.

They were just trying to make conversation, Cassie says. I'm always telling you not to go looking for trouble.

Do I look like I want to play Cluedo and talk about pop music?

They were just being friendly.

A knock sounds.

Hi, Toby says, when Cassie answers. I wondered if, er, if Miriam might …

Miriam appears at Cassie's side and Cassie edges back into

the room, sits on her bunk.

I thought you might want to go for a walk. It's a fantastic evening, Toby continues.

Who might?

Well, you, I mean …

I thought you had a girlfriend?

I did, I mean we split up recently.

And I look like her?

Yeah, a bit, I …

You said I look really like her earlier, didn't you?

Sorry, I didn't mean to …

Cassie, I'm going for a walk, see you later.

The door closes abruptly and Cassie stares at the wall opposite her bunk. Miriam? she asks the empty room. She sits in silence for long minutes before reaching for her ancient copy of *Jane Eyre*, a small hardback that smells of secondhand damp.

When Miriam returns she is smiling and secretive.

I think I'm getting a headache, she claims. I'm going to try to get to sleep before those awful girls come back. Tell them to be quiet when they get in.

She turns her back on Cassie in the bunk opposite. Cassie returns to *Jane Eyre* and raises a finger to her lips when the others return, nodding towards Miriam's sleeping form.

They pull faces and one sticks out her tongue at Miriam's back, but they tiptoe round the room and climb into their beds gingerly. Cassie turns off her reading torch and settles into the lumpy bed, the nylon of her inner bag static against her legs.

She wakes to the soft click of the dorm door closing, half sits. Miriam? she whispers.

She just left, a sleep-sodden voice from the bunk above her says.

Oh, she might be ill. I'd better …

Cassie pulls on a thin dressing gown flung across the bottom of her bed and scuttles to the washroom. There is no sign of Miriam. She tiptoes along the corridor, past the boys' dormitory and the family rooms. There is no-one in the sitting room, no-one in the kitchen. She considers going into the garden, wonders if she should get dressed. The warden emerges from a door marked 'no entry' beside the kitchen.

Is there a problem?

I … I can't find my friend. She's not in the dorm or anywhere I've looked. She gets ill sometimes … epilepsy, so …

Dark-haired girl?

Yes, Miriam. Miriam Jacobs.

I'll take a look in the garden. You're sure she's not inside?

I've looked everywhere. Except the other bedrooms, of course.

The warden, an older version of Toby, skin more weathered

around his grey eyes, nods and goes outside. Cassie moves from one foot to the other in the hallway, feeling the pre-dawn chill.

No-one out there, he says when he returns. You absolutely sure she wasn't in the toilet?

I'll look again.

After the next search, the warden says he'll fetch Toby so they can start looking beyond the hostel garden. Cassie scurries to the dorm, grabs yesterday's clothes in the gloom and carries them to the washroom. As she makes her way back to the front hallway she hears a roar, a rumpus of voices, Miriam's amongst them.

The warden emerges from the 'no entry' doorway, Miriam pushed ahead of him, dishevelled and weeping.

Miriam?

I want you out.

But …

Sorry, you'll have to ask your friend why you're being turfed out.

Miriam hunches her shoulders and skitters down the corridor, Cassie following. They pack in silence. The warden stands at the door, closes it firmly as they leave.

Miriam?

It was nothing.

We got thrown out for nothing? You were with Toby?

Yes. But it's not what you think. Just leave it, Cassie.

I think you …

No. I said leave it.

Miriam pulls her bike from the rack.

At least we'll get to see the sunrise, Miriam says, as she tugs her bike free and wheels it towards the road.

Cassie says nothing, pulls her bike towards her and follows.

And the roads will be really empty at this time, Miriam adds, trying to smile.

Cassie remains silent, mounts her bike, pushes away from the hostel and begins to pedal into the lane. But the air is warm and the green scents of mosses and ferns rise up and she relaxes.

It's so beautiful, Cassie calls over her shoulder after they have been pedalling for ten minutes.

Miriam waves and grins, and Cassie slows to let her catch up. They cycle side by side down the narrow lane until they turn onto a larger road, Miriam taking the lead again.

Cassie eases into the downhill surge of speed, relishes the cool breeze as the sun climbs in the sky, warming.

Watch out! Miriam calls, turning round to look at the coach approaching. Dragon approaching, Cassie! Hold your course!

Cassie smiles back at Miriam. We're not afraid of dragons, she calls back. She shifts her grip on the handlebars, checks she is not too close to the ditch, notices how much less tense she is on the bike today.

The coach moves out, slips past with plenty of room.

In front, Miriam wobbles slightly, but rights herself, continues straight before she lurches, yelling as she tumbles into the ditch just as the coach clears her and pulls further into the roadside.

Miriam!

Cassie hears the thin wail of the coach's breaks, a hiss of air as it comes to rest and the doors fold open, the driver emerging, followed by several passengers, Americans who exclaim, Oh, my and Goodness, shaking their heads.

I didn't hit her, the driver tells Cassie as she runs towards him, her bike discarded. I'm sure I didn't …

No, you didn't hit her, but we need to reach her.

Yes, of course. The driver peers into the ditch where Miriam is whimpering, pinioned on brambles, blood and purple juice mingling in runnels along her arms and legs.

The driver and two stocky American men slowly extricate Miriam, delivering her into the arms of a posse of women who produce tissues, even salve, and begin fussing meticulously. Oh, my goodness, darling. We'll soon have you right.

While the women work, the men disentangle the bike from the ditch.

Wheel's buckled, one says, holding the gnarled wreckage upright.

We'll take you home, darlings, one of the women offers.

Where do you live, sweetheart?

Teesside, Miriam whispers, beginning to cry silently, tears and mucous spreading across her face.

The American woman looks towards the driver, quizzical. Is that far? she burs.

Er … the driver looks like a trapped animal.

It's okay, Cassie interjects, we're staying with Miriam's sister in Keswick.

The driver's shoulders fall. No problem, he confirms. It's on our way.

They are bustled into the coach, offered sweets, 'cookies' and plied with questions, while the men load the bikes into the luggage compartment beneath the coach.

Until death, it's all life, Miriam whispers to Cassie as the coach pulls away towards Sarah's house.

November 1977

The unreason of the world is more insane than any fiction.

The first national strike of firefighters, demands for a wage increase of 30%.

British Airways inaugurate regular Concorde flights between London and New York.

Abba topple Baccara's 'Yes Sir I Can Boogie' to reach No.1 with 'That's the Name of the Game'.

And now for the weather: A showery month with sunny spells. Heavier rain and sleet is expected to fall in the north with some hail showers.

If You Could Read My Mind
December 1977

The story's dire.

Cassie laughs. Like one of Mandy's Mills and Boon books you mean?

Quite. Really, Casilda, awful. Tell me again.

I play Clara. She lives in this run down castle with her family and she's engaged to a local lawyer's son, Lawrence.

Very Dodie Smith, so derivative.

No, it's not set then and … it's not at all like *I Capture the Castle*. Just listen, Miriam. Anyway, at night Clara hears these noises. They wake her every night, scary noises, rustling at first, then louder, like chains clanging and she can't stand it any longer so she takes a torch and goes looking. In the oldest part of the castle, beyond the rooms that are habitable, she finds boards covering a hole and the noise is coming from there so she starts pulling at them and there's a well hidden underneath. When she shines the torch down the hole, someone calls up to her. She faints and wakes up back in bed so she thinks it's a dream, but later she finds her torch where she dropped it the night before and there's the well with the boards pulled loose so she goes back the next night and, standing by the well, is a ghost. He's beautiful, angelic-looking, but his feet are in chains and when she reaches out to him, he vanishes. The next night she goes back and he holds out a hand to warn her not to touch him and tells her his story. He's committed a terrible crime, killed someone long ago and he can only be redeemed and become human again by saving someone from a violent death. Anyway, she goes back each night and each night he becomes less ghostly, more substantial and she's falling in love with him, but in the daytime she's with Lawrence and they're planning their wedding. Lawrence is a nasty piece of work, by the way. When he's not with Clara we see him with this friend, Peter, telling him that there is treasure under the castle and once he's married Clara it will be his. That's why he's marrying her.

Oh, for goodness sake, Cassie, you can't be serious.

Cassie laughs. It's local amateur dramatics, Miriam, not Brecht or Beckett. One of the group leaders wrote it. I know it's corny, but the acting is fun. Really. Anyway, one night, Lawrence visits Clara late after work to tell her he has to go away for a few days because of a family emergency and he discovers her with the ghost.

No phones at this castle?

Apparently not. Lawrence assumes the worst and runs towards Clara, hand raised to hit her and she steps back and falls into the well. The ghost saves her …

Of course he does.

But Lawrence tumbles in and is killed in the fall.

How convenient.

You'd think. Cassie stifles a giggle.

The ghost, Oliver by name, becomes a real boy and plans to marry Clara.

And they all live happily ever after?

No, that's the thing. Turns out Oliver has had the same plan as Lawrence all along. He's just after the treasure, which is how he came to kill someone the first time round, so Clara is in big danger.

Gordon Bennett! So much betrayal. I suppose you'll betray me one day.

Don't be silly, Miriam. Anyway, enter Edward.

Who?

He's a local guy who's into history. He comes to talk to Clara's family about the history of the castle. He tells them the story of how the daughter of a former owner had been murdered by her lover after he'd stolen the family valuables. The murderer, Oliver Saxonby, disappeared soon after, but rumours persisted that the haul was still hidden at the castle. Everyone is a bit uneasy that the murderer had the same name as Clara's fiancé, especially Clara, who knows that he was recently a ghost who had killed someone.

She never thought to ask who he murdered?

It's not that kind of story. Anyway …

They're all saved by Edward.

Au contraire, ma sœur. Cassie splutters back laughter. Oliver has overheard everything, including Clara telling Edward privately that she's worried about 'her own' Oliver. She doesn't say he used to be a ghost, of course. Oliver tells Clara that Edward sounds really interesting and gets her to invite him to a family dinner. He secretly poisons the food and the final scene's like Shakespearian slaughter but without the iambic pentameter.

Also without the writing or plot, Miriam adds.

You speak the truth, but be quiet. Having killed them all, Oliver knows where to hide the bodies: in the bowels of the castle. Then he digs up the treasure and wins the day. *Quelle tragédie.*

It's a tragedy for narrative everywhere, I'll say that. So you get to die horribly?

I do.

The person who wrote this should be shot for crimes against humanity.

You haven't heard the best yet.

Oh, God, no! There can't be more.

Cassie laughs. The inspiration is a Gordon Lightfoot song. I thought me and Sean were the only people in the world who listened to him. I'm acting in a Gordon Lightfoot song, well a rather mangled version of one, anyway.

Let me guess which one. Miriam pauses. 'If you could read my mind'?

Got it in one.

Good grief! Cheap romance, Cassie. What have I told you about romance? Head rot. Dangerous stuff. Unbelievable. Are you brilliant in the part?

I think I do okay.

I'm sure you're stunning. Good. This is what we need, Casilda. Distraction and obfuscation. Play your part, my sweet saint. The mask is your protection. No-one will ever track you down while you hide in the carnival. The unreason of this age is madder than any fiction, after all.

Yes, Cassie says. Yes.

He's been in her dreams for over a year now. The beach goes on forever, a boundary of coarse sand and marram grass further from the tide line, beyond which is forestry, pine trees shading brown needles and stories of lost children. There is no one else walking here, a mile, two miles from the caravan site. They walk where the sand is wet, the shuck of bare feet on grains moist with salt and sea. Cassie watches the footprints, Miriam's slightly wider, longer. She is dressed in transparent cheesecloth floating from her thin torso on breaths of sea breeze, cotton skirt edged in lace.

And so I brought your cure when you were weak, almost dead, Casilda, Miriam is saying. I sought out the Christian talisman that would restore your health, knowing that you had secretly given your heart to Christ, risking your father's wrath. I made a vow then to return to the religion of my fathers, to the God of Abraham, Isaac and Jacob, if the relic cured you, if you lived. When I arrived in Toledo your father was beyond himself with grief. I had a hard time persuading King Alamun to allow me even one minute alone with you and your nurse. You were so pale that for a moment I thought I'd come too late, but your eyes flickered and you told me you had been expecting me. I had brought you a scrap of the Virgin's robe, dipped in holy water, and I knew that if you had found faith you would live. You said simply, I believe, and you were well again. It wasn't the relic;

not magic, but faith that healed you, Casilda. Belief is your gift. I believe, you said, and you were laughing and well and then Alamun and his men were in the room, swords drawn, amazed to see you sitting up, healthy and happy.

I knew the price of saving you would be terrible. That I would be betrothed to your sister Zoraida as a reward, that I could not refuse the powerful Alamun and his son Ahmed, my allies. I was like Abraham commanded to kill his son. I had been commanded to put aside my love for Casilda in order to save Casilda, to save you.

Miriam slips an arm around her waist, pulls her close. God always demands sacrifice, my Casilda, even after saying he's through with it.

He is there, in the dream, walking beside them, chatting about the weather, the town, how long have they been in Nairn, where are they from, how they like it here, are their parents near by, they don't look like sisters.

Cassie watches the footprints in the sand. The caravan site is further and further behind them. There is no one else on the beach. Only six footprints going on and on at the shoreline, his large, splayed. He wears blue swimming trunks, points to a boat far out towards the horizon, moves between them as they stop to look. His arm is around Cassie, his hand is sticky. Just do what I say, he tells her. Do what I say and you'll be fine. The blue swimming trunks are on the sand, little waves nibbling at them. She can't make sense. And Miriam? The man turns with Cassie in his grasp so that she lurches against him, the sticky hand slipping on her bare arm, pulling tighter. She has seen only smooth sand going on and on, but Miriam has a rock, jagged and dark. She holds it like a small rugby ball. No, Miriam says. No. She lifts both arms, hurls the rock, Cassie flinches away and the man looses his grasp, gasps, swears and they are running towards the dry sand and marram grass, towards the forest, but Miriam is slower and he's tall and muscled and has her in grasp, shaking her.

Run, Cassie, run!

Cassie turns, sees him pull Miriam hard towards him. Sees him pause, flinch from the hum rising to a howl, the sound that Cassie knows marks the margin between ecstasy and unconsciousness. She watches Miriam fall from his hold, watches him toe her roughly, lean over her slumped body, tug on her skirt, blue and red daisies flecked with sand.

She runs, not away, but back towards Miriam. God always demands sacrifice. Sand wails beneath feet. The rock in her hands, heavy, uneven. A Sunday school picture of Abraham about to sacrifice his son, because God had commanded it. Belief is your gift. The ram in the thicket. The man leans over Miriam, blue and red daisies on cream cotton tossed in the sand. The rock moves towards him, glances his thigh. He lopes after her, hand rubbing the red mark, face scarlet, screaming words she can't sense, mouth contorted, vicious, sound-track cut, heat hazes the sand, hands close around neck, ragged breath, white cotton tearing. She falls onto sand, wakes filmed in sour-milk sweat.

He's been in her dreams for over a year, never reaching the end. The story and the facts don't match.

Meet the world on Teesside, the international eisteddfod poster proclaims as they arrive, wind-swept and dishevelled on the steps of Middlesbrough town hall. From beyond the crested double doors, a brass band begins to play. Miriam wrinkles her nose, shoves the door open.

Let's get out of this hail. Where's your event?

The Crypt.

Nice. Miriam shakes her coat off, smoothes down her red dress. Mine's upstairs in a committee room. I will no doubt sit through scores of awful renditions of 'That's An Irish Lullaby' before I perform.

Good luck.

It's not luck I need, Cassie. I sing so much better when you're with me. Do you really have to abandon me?

Cassie hesitates, looks down, flushed. It's just … I mean I've been rehearsing with Jill for ages and I'm her best student. I'll come up as soon as I'm finished.

You're bound to miss me. It's only poetry, Cassie. And I'm not sure those elocution lessons are having much effect on you in any case.

It's the performing I like. And my mam has paid the entry fee. There'll be blood if I don't do it now. Cassie moves from foot to foot, rubs her hands together.

Oh, well if you must. How many times down the centuries have I saved your life, Casilda? As Ben Haddaj of course, and before that and later …

I think my event starts in a minute.

Miriam turns, flounces towards the stairs.

Good luck, Cassie says to her retreating back.

Cassie pauses. The Farjeon piece is too simple, she thinks, but Jill had chosen the poems for her to perform. She can see the kingcup gatherer before her as she begins the poem about him, flowers in a basket crowning him, flames of yellow. Behind a table spread with a starched linen cloth, three judges whisper to one another, make notes, nod to her to begin her second piece. She wonders how Miriam is faring, begins the Tessimond — the sinuous fluidity of cats, their inability to be owned, the sibilant syllables flowing. She remembers wanting to be called Kat when she was at infant school, wanting not to be less than herself like Tessimond's cats.

Thank you, dear. One of the judges smiles. And your final piece?

Cassie begins the Preludes, relaxes into Eliot's rhythm, the taste of his words, the chime of repetitions, the ache they leave resonating —

She runs up the stairs, pauses at the door in case someone is mid-song. Quiet. She edges the handle down, pushes gently. Miriam is walking to the stage as she slips into a seat at the back. She smiles as Miriam turns, hands her music to the pianist. Miriam tilts her head to one side, black hair swinging above a scarlet dress.

Mag dir, du zartes Frühlings-kind,
dies erste Blümchen fromen.
Oh take, thou lovely child of Spring,
this Spring's first tender flower.

In the summing up the judges commend the young lady who had chosen a more challenging song, note that she'd learned the Grieg in German, which was to be encouraged in young singers, awarded first and third place to two renditions of 'That's An Irish Lullaby' and second place to a plump girl in a too tight pink dress who'd sung 'Early One Morning'.

Metumtam, Miriam hisses, nodding towards the main judge, who is now thanking the audience for listening so graciously. She slumps next to Cassie at the back of the room, holding a highly commended certificate as though it harbours disease. *Shtok, ya metumtam.*

Shh, Miriam, he'll hear you.

Miriam shakes her head, black hair belling around an angry face. And you?

Oh, it was fine.

You mean you came first in your class?

Yes.

Like a show dog. Didn't they give you a ribbon? I suppose poetry's just easier. She sighs, leans her head briefly against Cassie's shoulder. I'm starving. Let's find Judith. She's stewarding somewhere, but she has sandwiches and cake. I need cake.

He's been in her dreams for over a year now. The beach goes on forever …

January 1978

The unreason of the world is more insane than any fiction.

After three months, the firefighters strike comes to an end with the acceptance of a 10% pay increase and shorter working hours.

The UK Government is found guilty of mistreating prisoners in Northern Ireland by The European Court of Human Rights, but cleared of charges of torture.

Margaret Thatcher, leader of the opposition, speaks out for Britons who fear being *swamped by people with a different culture.*

The Yorkshire Ripper claims his eighth victim – an eighteen-year-old prostitute, Helen Rytka – is that a British name? Could half-Jamaican women swamp the culture?

Wings reach No.1 with 'Mull of Kintyre', so much more reassuring.

And now for the weather: The month will be unsettled with wintry showers including hail, sleet and snow. There are likely to be heavy falls of snow in the north. It will be generally wet with risk of blizzards, fog and severe conditions.

Song for a Winter's Night
January 1978

We must be heroic in the face of reality, Cassie.

I know, but …

No buts. We live in an insane world. Apparent insanity is the only sane response. And if we had to go to that ridiculous event, then I needed to make my mark.

Cassie nods uncertainly.

Judith thinks I should have protected you or should have stopped you wearing that outfit. She's going to cause a lot of fuss at college.

Good.

Do you like having enemies?

It's not a matter of liking it, Cassie, it's sometimes inevitable.

Cassie stops herself from saying that none of it was inevitable. That now she will be starting their second term at sixth form alone. The doctor has insisted Miriam must rest for at least a week after such an extreme episode, but Miriam looks triumphant despite the dark shadows under her eyes.

Cassie closes her eyes on the images of New Year's Eve. She doubts they will be invited to any more parties.

Cassie had knocked at the stout wooden door. A Christmas wreath crisp with ice hung above the letterbox. Behind them Mr Jacobs sat in his car, engine still running, watching until they were safely inside. She listened to the laughter inside, a swollen winter door being tugged open.

Cassie, hi, come in and Miriam.

Joanne's face was flushed to match her hair. She wore a long navy skirt, a gypsy top embroidered in reds and blues. Cassie took off her coat and handed it to Joanne.

Nice dress, Joanne complimented.

Cassie smoothed down the pale blue maxi crimpelene, smiled.

Shall I take your coat, Miriam?

Miriam slowly undid the belt of her school gabardine, turned her back on Cassie and Joanne to undo the buttons and wriggle free before presenting the coat to Joanne with a flourish.

That's … that's really different, Joanne said.

I am different, Miriam assented.

Oh my gawd, look at that, Penny said loudly as Cassie and Miriam followed Joanne into the living room.

I'm going to wet my knickers, Sally added, holding her stomach and falling onto the floor, laughter rolling in tears.

Would you like something to drink … or eat? Joanne asked, waving an uncertain hand towards a table in the corner of the room arranged with tiny sausages and pineapple on sticks, crustless egg sandwiches, bottles of lemonade in assorted sticky colours.

Cassie sidled towards the table, head down, spilled pink globs of cherryade on the white cloth as she poured shakily.

Miriam made a bow.

It's not bloody fancy dress, you know, Penny said.

But Penny, it's New Year's Eve, a time for decorum and dignity, surely? Miriam retorted, unfazed.

You look a right idiot, Penny countered.

Miriam stood in the centre of the room, defiant in her black three-piece man's suit, white shirt, red dickey-bow. Sally was still giggling, curled up on the floor. The other girls watched Penny and Miriam, facing each other like dogs about to attack.

Cassie held her breath, but Miriam took a step back, smiled, turned and left the room.

Ha! Good riddance, Penny called after her. Stupid cow — or is it sow? Stupid Jew-sow!

Cassie put down her drink, but before she could follow, Miriam had returned, flushed, but smiling still.

Shouldn't have left these in my pocket, she said, waving a

pair of man's leather driving gloves.

She marched forward, raised the gloves, whipped them across Penny's face to an intake of breath from the watching girls, brought them down harder on the other cheek.

Consider yourself challenged, Miss Dean, she hissed, dropping the gloves at Penny's feet.

Penny coloured, a hand going to her cheek. You pigging freak! Her hand raised higher and came down hard across the side of Miriam's head. Penny grabbed a handful of dark hair and wrenched Miriam to her knees, pushed her backwards.

Penny! Joanne moved forward, then back, uncertain. Around the room girls shrank back or laughed nervously. Mam! Dad! Joanne shouted, dashing from the room.

Cassie knocked the whole drink over, pink on the pale carpet, as she launched towards Miriam on the floor, right arm beginning to twitch.

No! She fended off Penny's next blow. She's having an attack.

Penny shrank back as the wailing sound rose from Miriam's curled body.

Sally sat up. I think I'm going to hurl.

One of the watching girls began to cry.

With the furthest to drive, Mr Jacobs was the last of the fathers to arrive to collect a shaken, unhappy daughter. Cassie's father had already lost his job by then and had taken another in the Middle East, like so many men made redundant from ICI and British Steel, so she had no choice but to wait with Miriam, Joanne, and her shocked parents.

You're sure she'll be all right? Joanne's mother asked.

Yes. She'll be fine, but it can take a while before she's really here again.

Miriam lay on the pale carpet, a towel under her head, too late to catch the thin stream of vomit. She was quiet now, but moaned occasionally as the slow minutes oozed by.

You are sure she'll be all right? Joanne's mother asked again.

Cassie nodded and Miriam said something indistinct.

Shh. It's okay. Your dad will be here soon.

I see you all from a great height, Miriam slurred. Mere mortals, so outmoded. Doomed, of course.

It's okay, Mrs Leigh, Cassie tried to reassure. Her brain gets muddled when she's coming round. She isn't always sure who she is for a bit, but it soon passes.

I am an immortal, Miriam said in a louder monotone. I have lived hundreds of lives and will persist when you are worm food. All but you, my darling Casilda.

Oh, dear, Mrs Leigh said. Oh, dear.

I've loved you through the ages, my sweet saint. Miriam began to sob. Do you hear that? Run, Casilda! Run. Don't let them take you. No! No!

Mrs Leigh began to pace the floor as the doorbell rang.

Cassie crouched by Miriam. Shh. Shh, your dad's here now. You'll soon be feeling better.

It will never be better. Miriam's sobs choked the next words into guttural blurs. Never. Never. I have to put this right, Casilda, all of it. Don't you understand? I have to … she curled into herself, wailing.

I've got to go, Cassie says.

Really? I wish you could stay.

Judith said only a short visit and I've got homework to finish and …

And what? Miriam sits up in bed. You didn't agree to it, did you?

Cassie nods.

Betrayal. All I ever want is you, Casilda, but I'm never enough for you, am I?

Don't be silly, it's just …

You are all I need to get me through this long winter. It's simple for me.

I promised at the end of last term. The first debate's in week and I'm leading the team.

I'm not coming to watch.

Okay, Cassie says quietly.

Drop out.

Cassie hesitates. I can't.

You mean you won't. You won't do this small thing for me.

I promised.

Cassie hears Judith on the stairs.

I've got to go. I'll come again soon. Get better fast.

Cassie is at the door before Judith opens it. Judith purses thin lips as Cassie edges past her, follows her downstairs.

I've been hiding those awful books, Judith says as Cassie crosses the hallway towards the kitchen and the back door.

Sorry?

All those romances putting ridiculous ideas into her head. I've been hiding them. But this one … In here …

Judith goes into the kitchen, holds the door open for Cassie. On the scrubbed oak table are three copies of *Casilda of the Rising Moon*.

This is the one, isn't it? This is who she thinks you are?

I … I don't … I mean …

Never mind. I'm taking no chances. If you have any sense you'll get rid of yours too. And stop encouraging this … this nonsense. You can see what it's doing to her, Cassie.

Judith carries the copies of *Casilda* out into the garden, Cassie following, watching from the patio as Judith picks her way along the line of broken paving slabs meandering across the lawn. Near the back fence a small bonfire smoulders. Judith tosses the copies into the desultory flames that spark and lick as the pages curl, blacken and collapse.

Cassie holds back a cry, turns, makes her way out of the side gate and begins to run.

June 1978

The unreason of the world is more insane than any fiction.

Naomi James – first woman to sail around the world single-handedly.

A general election is expected this autumn as Callaghan's minority government nears the end of its time. The Conservative's eleven-point lead evaporates; Callaghan's chances looking stronger.

A civilian and three members of the IRA die in a shoot-out between British Army and Provisional IRA.

After five weeks at No.1, Boney M's 'Rivers of Babylon' is toppled by Olivia Newton John and John Travolta with 'You're the One That I Want'.

And now for the weather: Despite the likelihood of warm periods at the beginning of the month, June will be unsettled, with outbursts of heavy rain, thunderstorms and overnight fog, which will persist in coastal areas.

The Circle is Small
June 1978

Cassie looks into the function room, shudders. She lays the bouquet of wilting rose buds on a side table and breathes deeply, wishing Miriam had agreed to come to the wedding.

Oh Casilda, I would, my sweet princess, but really — all that disco music and the crowd — I'd be bound to have an episode, spoil it for you. Be brave, Cassie. It's just one day.

Cassie pulls at the stiff fabric of her polyester satin bridesmaid dress, puffed sleeves clench her upper arm and the beetroot fabric rustles stiffly as she moves. Around the room eleven cousins of various ages flaunt the same bull-enchanting shade in assorted shapes. Her legs prickle in nylon tights and she feels unsteady on the carmine wedge sandals that Mandy insisted on.

At the far side of the room a DJ, thinning grey hair held back in a greasy ponytail, is setting up a stack of discs and beginning his patter into a microphone that screeches resistance every few seconds.

That's not the look of someone who's happy to be here. Liam is beside her. Sorry, can't tell a lie. He laughs.

Thanks. Cassie smiles.

Well at least the meal is over.

And the speeches.

Fuck, yes, pardon my French. But, really? Sorry, but your uncle Pat crying as he swayed to the beat of: love her tender or I'll hunt you down and gut you like a dog — now that was really something else.

Yes. Welcome to the family.

Not that close, Liam says. I mean … I don't mean I wouldn't want you as family. Just, we're not … you know … not like really related or anything … I mean if we wanted … you know … Anyway, I'll catch you later.

Cassie watches Liam scurry away. Under one of the tables two small bridesmaids and a pageboy are pooling drinks from a dozen unfinished glasses, passing the resulting concoction between them. She sees one of her aunts notice the trio, elbow her sister, both of them laughing together. Aw, sweet, she lip-reads.

The DJ slides his mouth around the microphone, Ladies and Gentlemen, please give the floor to the lovely couple, Mr and Mrs Sean and Amanda Brennan.

Sean walks to the centre of the room, as though he's expecting a firing squad. Amanda's mascara has run down her right cheek, the powder caking in the June humidity. She grins, sniffs back a tear.

Aw, lovely, Aunty Sue shouts into the space. An uncle wolf-whistles.

And a special number for a very special couple.

Sean and Mandy waltz to 'Three Times a Lady', Cassie

musing about coming to the end of the rainbow on the first day of their marriage.

During the applause Christopher Walters appears at her side to ask her to dance. Marcia's dancing with someone else, he says glumly.

Cassie makes it through 'Heart of Glass', wondering if the DJ has listened to any of the lyrics he plays at weddings, mutters apologies to Christopher when the assembled hoards begin lining up to perform 'Summer Nights'.

She finds a pay phone near the toilets, rings Miriam's number, Redcar 72953. The phone trills, on and on, on and on until the note changes to a monotone buzz. No one home. She begins to dial again, puts down the receiver, walks outside and sits on the wall, the hot June day becoming a sticky evening, clouds massing over the gare, gulls screaming, flare stacks and cooling towers to her left, the sea ahead, the sun beginning to set on the grey line of horizon.

Miriam, come with me, it sounds interesting.

Miriam had shaken her head. If you want to meet new people, that's up to you, Cassie, but you'll find they're as dull as everyone else. Voice brittle, she hadn't looked up from the Borges' story she was reading. Listen to this, Cassie. 'Historical truth, for Menard, is not "what happened"; it is what we *believe* happened.'

You sure you won't come?

Are you listening to me, Cassie? This is important.

Sorry. I just thought. Liam says they have a lot of political discussions and take part in boycotts and stuff. No-one in the group buys anything from Nestlé or from South Africa and …

You don't need 'and stuff', Cassie.

What?

You mean 'pardon?'. I'm trying to help you speak properly. I'd better complete your education before you run off and leave me.

What? Sorry, pardon. Miriam, I'm just going to a youth group to see what it's like. They've been reading the *Caucasian Chalk Circle* together — taking the parts and discussing it. Don't you think that's interesting?

Perhaps. I suppose you can check it out for us, but it's hardly a youth group. We'd be the youngest there. Anyway, we've only just started sixth form. We don't need distractions, especially you.

Why especially me?

Goodness, Cassie. You are argumentative today. Three A levels, that rather dodgy am-dram group, debating society and teaching Sunday School, if you need a list. You're already doing too much.

I'm fine. And they sound interesting. A lot of them are graduates. Or dropped out.

So they're old hippies?

No — there's a guy called Alex who lives at The House. He helped lead a rent strike at university — Warwick, I think — a couple of years ago and they ended up occupying the Senate House and then he decided to leave, become an anarchist …

Oh, Cassie, I'm not sure about these people; maybe it's not a good idea. You know how easily swayed you can be.

I'm going this Sunday, Cassie had said quietly, as Miriam's right arm began to tremble so slightly it might be a trick of the light.

Cassie, eh? Excellent. I always know I'm going to like someone when she has her name embroidered across her chest. Very Dadaist.

Cassie glanced down at her dungarees, her name in red lazy daisy stitch on the bib.

Welcome, Cassie, keeper of the fluid line between art and life. I'm Alex. Cassie had shifted uneasily as Alex, lank red hair flopping forward, stooped to grip her in a bear hug. Welcome to The House.

It was eleven o'clock before she realised she'd missed the last bus back from Saltburn.

Plenty of spare beds, Zoë told her. Me and Alex are in the attic. Stevie has the back room by the bathroom, best for nights on the piss. Frank's in the big room at the front, so take your pick of the others. The one next to Stevie is cosiest.

Yeah, we were thinking of staying over too, Lorraine put in, grinning at her taciturn boyfriend, Tim. She'd looked at Cassie as she asked, What about you, Liam?

Liam glanced in Cassie's direction. I think that's all rooms taken, but I can get a lift with Terry, yeah?

Yeah, but I'd better get going, got a mechanics paper to finish.

Jack it in, man. What you going to do with a maths degree from Teesside Poly anyway? Alex asked.

God knows, teach maths I suppose.

Oppressor! Alex boomed, but laughed instantly. You should be out toiling like Liam here, one of the workers.

Workers? He only got the job cos his dad's a manager, commented Jeremy, a stringy history student who never seemed to put down his guitar. That's how come he can afford that fancy instrument while I have to make do with this. He waved his guitar, strummed more chords, ignored the paper dart that Liam winged in his direction. One more round of 'Alice's Restaurant' for the road?

So where were we? Alex asked when the chorus subsided and Terry, Liam and two blonde girls, both called Diane, had left.

Gianfranco Sanguinetti, Cassie replied.

Yeah, so him and Debord were basically last men standing, but he went out fighting — he wrote this spoof pamphlet as though it came from some capitalist wanker— then he got all these politicians supporting it, saying that a big bombing in Milan that killed a load of people had been worth it to make people think it was done by lefties and anarchists so they'd go on supporting capitalism. Then, while they're all praising this pamphlet, over five hundred of the fuckers, Sangiunetti comes out and tells them he wrote it to set them up. *Quel scandale.* He had to get out of Italy, but they wouldn't let him back in France so he holed up in Greece for a bit. So, that's Sanguinetti, but I lost the thread on Jorn a while back, yeah?

Cassie nodded.

Alex, you've had Cassie pinned down listening to you for four hours, Zoë said, tousling his long hair. She might need a break, sweetie.

Yeah? Sorry, Cassie, captive audience. But remind me to tell you about the Frankfurt School sometime, yeah?

Miriam will like The House, Cassie thought as she shook out a musty smelling patchwork bedspread in the spare room, yawning.

Okay, folks, group meeting in ten, Alex had called, depositing a box of groceries in the small kitchen. Is that the last?

Zoë rummaged in the box. Looks like, yeah. Here you go, Cassie. She handed contents to Cassie who was perched on a ladder to fill an overhead cupboard with supplies. Are there candles inside? And torches? If the weather closes in we might need them.

Cosy, Alex said, grinning. Couple of pots of tea for the meeting?

Any biccies? Liam asked, putting his head round the door, dark curls flopping.

Biccies? Are you ten? But yes, we can run to that. Jeremy wanted to know if you brought your guitar?

Wearisome can keep his hands off.

Don't call him that, Zoë shot back. Anyway, he plays it well — the guitar must like it.

Guitars don't have opinions, Liam corrected. This one cost

me a month's wages and it's in perfect nick. I've seen the way Wearisome throws his guitar around.

That's cos it's an old wreck. I'm sure he'd be careful with yours.

Course I would, Jeremy added behind Liam. I'll cherish every mother of pearl and gold piece on it. Just let me make it sing for a change.

Tosser, Liam said.

We're all tossers, man, but at least I can play.

In the dining room of the bunkhouse attached to Osmotherley's Quaker Meeting House, the group huddled round the large round table nursing cups of tea. Liam dunked biscuits and sucked noisily, grinning at Jeremy's disapproval.

Okay, folks, this is the deal. The good Friends have let us use this place really cheap so we need to respect their rules, right? That means we've got boys dorms in here and the girls are in the attic room with the double and two singles. Any objections?

Lorraine pouted, tossed a long strand of chestnut hair and looked at Tim, who buried his face in a mug of tea.

That's fine, Zoë agreed. Cassie, Miriam, you okay in the double? At least you'll have a chance of keeping warm. Everyone should make sure they've got access to a torch and there are plenty of candles, but let's not burn the place down. Oh … Zoë stopped, looking out of the window. Oh, look.

They turned to watch thin flakes of snow thickening fast.

I knew this was a bad idea, Liam said.

Yeah? So what you doing here then? Jeremy asked. Snowball fight's in an hour, he announced. You up for it, Cassie? You're on my team. Who's with Liam?

Liam scowled. Tosser. We'd better not get snowed in is all. I've got work on Monday. Maybe we should go back now.

No, a chorus came.

Two hours later, muffled in a thick Icelandic sweater, scarf, hat, mittens, Cassie was outside with Zoë, Alex, Jeremy, Stevie and Tim, hurling snowballs, running and screeching. Liam ventured out briefly, looked thunderous when Jeremy began a game of 'pass the Cassie', lifting her like a sack before throwing her forward, calling, Catch Alex, who in turn called, At Stevie. Lorraine huddled in the doorway, complained about the bitter cold, went in to sit with Miriam by the window, before calling Tim back inside from the 'infantile games'.

Don't spaz out and give in, Jeremy said when Tim obediently ambled into the almost warm kitchen.

Tim grinned weakly, shrugged.

Hey, Lorraine, how about making hot chocolate if you're not coming out? Jeremy called, lobbing a large snowball overarm at Liam, who had reappeared to check his car engine would still turn over.

Fat chance, Lorraine called back.

Later, all of them huddled as close as possible to the small open fire in the long living room, Jeremy playing 'All Along the Watchtower' on Liam's shiny guitar with its strange plastic back, Liam reached a hand around Cassie's shoulder.

You know you're beautiful, he whispered.

Cassie squirmed, watched Miriam stand, cross the short space between them, reach out both hands to hers to pull her up. There's something I want to show you, Miriam said, tugging.

In the tiny attic bedroom with its three beds pushed up close to each other, Miriam pushed Cassie to sit and came alongside. What was that?

I'm not sure, Cassie admitted.

But unwelcome.

I don't know, Cassie said, wondering if she always had to be so truthful.

You don't know? You mean it might be? You and Liam Brennan? Aren't you already related to him?

Not really. He's my brother in law's cousin. And I simply mean I don't know. I've never really thought about him like that. Well …

Well?

Cassie coloured. Maybe at school. I don't know. He's very …

Needy, Miriam completed for her. He's needy, paranoid and moody.

You think? He was always kind at school. Funny sometimes.

And thick.

No, not thick. Just not … not academic I suppose. He's going to college for his job.

Day release. Sounds like something prisoners do. He's beneath you, Cassie.

He reads Viking sagas, Cassie said. And he talks to Alex about politics.

He never stops talking. Doesn't do much listening though. And he makes up rubbish all the time. I don't like him, Cassie. And I'm not feeling right.

What do you mean? An episode?

Perhaps. I'm not sure. Don't go back down. I need to be quiet. I don't want to be up here alone. Okay, Cassie? For me?

The next morning the snow had deepened. Great stuff, Jeremy enthused. Fancy coming to Mass with me, Cassie? Lovely walk through the village. Our Lady of Mount Grace.

Mass? Liam asked.

That'd be the one, my heathen friend.

I'm C of E actually, Liam retorted. Well, sort of C of E. I didn't know you were Catholic, Cassie.

Yes, she is. Cassie's a saint actually, Miriam put in. She's going to read theology at Oxford and become a leading mystic. You should go, Cassie. I'll be fine here. I'm going to help Zoë and Lorraine make pancakes for breakfast. We'll do them for when you get back.

I thought you were Jewish, Liam's voice was low and petulant. How come you're so keen on all this Catholic rot? Do you know how much misery that church is responsible for? In the third world? All that crap about no contraception. And don't get me started on Mother Teresa. What a fraud.

Thought your family were Irish Catholics, Jeremy retorted to Liam. But yeah, let's not get you started on religion bashing, eh? Coming Cassie?

I'll just get my hat and things. Are you sure you're okay, Miriam?

Yes, really. You go with Jeremy, angel. Miriam spoke looking at Liam, smiling more brightly than she had since they'd arrived in Osmotherley.

My dad's Catholic for your information, Liam muttered, but not my mam and I wasn't brought up with all that twaddle.

Don't think anyone's that bothered, Miriam said with relish. How's your car by the way, Liam?

Liam shook his head and stomped towards the kitchen.

In the fading dusk later that day, Liam fumbled with the engine while Jeremy held a torch.

It's not funny, Wearisome, Liam said for the third time. Try it again, Liam instructed Tim behind the wheel.

Nothing, Li.

Shit. Hold that torch higher, for fuck's sake.

Maybe we should phone Terry. Stevie hovered behind

Jeremy, moving from foot to foot to keep warm. It'll be dark soon. He glanced at his watch. 4.40, the light seeping into murkier grey. He could give you a tow.

I knew this was a bad idea, Liam said, slamming the bonnet down so that Jeremy had to jump backwards with the torch.

Miriam sat at the window, head resting on arms, watching, smiling. She turned to Cassie, reading *Tristram Shandy* on the sofa nearby. I do like this place, she said, sighing contentedly.

Penny for them.

Miriam startles. Behind her, the Coatham Bowl pulsates to 'Night Fever'.

You looked really far away, Liam says.

I was thinking about The House. The first time I went there and Alex talking to me for hours.

Yeah, he can do that.

He's not the only one, Cassie says, smiling.

Yeah, well. Liam shrugs.

And also about that weekend at Osmotherley when we got snowed in and your new mini wouldn't start.

Yeah, right faff on that was. That place was freezing and Wearisome was a pain in the proverbial all weekend, going on about my guitar. Someone should take the stick out of his … Sorry, not the moment … Liam runs a hand through brown curls, pauses. You looked really gorgeous staring off into the sunset like that.

Cassie laughs, tugs at the red polyester. In this?

In anything actually.

Oh.

Sorry. Well, no, not really — I mean … you do look gorgeous. Liam leans in, large hand on the nape of her neck beneath her hair, pulls her towards him, mouth seeking hers. Cassie gasps, twists, teeth clatter and she jerks back, shaking her head.

Right, Liam says, stepping backwards, snagging her hair as he looses his hand. Yeah. He turns away, walks back towards the Bowl, strains of 'Annie's Song' crooning to the early night through the open doors.

Cassie tucks her legs under her on the wall, rocks. The wind from the sea has a bite now that the sun has gone. Across the gare the lights of ICI and all the miles of industry beyond flicker and wink, sulphur and salt on the night air, a flare of fire from one of the Bunsen-burner like stacks that point into the sky, stars eclipsed by the haze of industry, lights of town after town. Cassie shivers, hops from the wall, walks towards the last bars of 'Annie's Song'.

In the vestibule, Sean is leaning against a wall, crying quietly.

Sean?

He turns, eyes filmed, forehead moist with sweat, his carmine cravat hangs loose over a half-unbuttoned shirt, white but for the faint tinge of beer splash to the left of his chest.

I'm not good enough for her, Cassie. I'll never be good enough for her. He begins to sob more noisily. And you ... he chokes, sniffs, wipes the back of his hand across his nose ... I shouldn't have done that to you ... tears flow, he shudders, gags ... At the stable last summer ... it's never been the same since ... I always loved you, Cassie ... not like ... you know ... but I ... oh, God, I'm such a fuck up, Cassie ... I don't ... don't know what to do ...

The sobs become a painful base note, deep wailing. Cassie looks towards the double doors of the main room where people sag on chairs, drunk, reminiscing, crying softly into bad beer and worse wine, a few stalwarts feign lack-lustre dance steps to 'Love is in the Air'.

Let's find somewhere quiet, she says.

In the back room, Cassie settles Sean onto a crimson velvet banquette, its stuffing spilling along frayed edges, fetches water, a cloth for him to dry his eyes. She sits on a bar stool in front of him.

It's just the wedding, Sean. A lot of emotion flying around. You're fine. Mandy adores you.

She thinks I'll make it, Sean says, head hanging.

You'll be fine. You'll pass your exams next time, be an accountant.

I fucking hate it, Cassie.

Oh, Sean. I thought ...

Sorry, it's not that bad, I suppose. It's just I always wanted to be a jockey. Since I was a kid. Couldn't keep my weight down, couldn't make the grade. So I ride out on Saturdays and knuckle down to become Mr Suburbia and give Mandy everything she wants. Everything she deserves. I know she does, it's just … You're not like her, are you?

I don't know if I'm like anyone. My mam has been telling me that as long as I can remember — no idea where I came from. When I was little I used to wonder if they were trying to tell me I'm adopted, but I look just like her so it's not that. It just freaks her out — the books I read, the music I listen to.

Gordon Lightfoot?

Cassie laughs. Wagner, Leoncavallo, the concerts Miriam takes me to.

She's a bit … a bit — odd, your friend, isn't she?

Intense. She sees the world in a certain way. Do you know Camus — *The Stranger*?

Sean guffaws. Do I look like I read that stuff?

Cassie smiles. Well there's this character called Mersault who does something terrible, kills someone, but he doesn't see it as wrong because it was his instinct — he believes he's always right, never second guesses himself. At his trial he has no remorse and says: 'I had been right, I was still right, I was always right.' Miriam knows she's right. It doesn't always make her easy. She sees the world the way she sees it and believes.

And you?

She's taught me a lot. I wouldn't be about to do Cambridge entrance exams without Miriam. I'd probably think I was a freak with nowhere to belong.

You'd be alright anywhere, Cassie, you're strong.

Perhaps.

No, really. You should believe in yourself.

Belief is my gift. Cassie laughs softly.

What's that?

It's something Miriam used to tell me. I think it's a gracious way of saying I'm gullible. She's right, though. I take things at face value. I believe what people tell me. I see the world through her eyes.

Empathy.

I suppose, but not just that.

You believe in God too? I mean, I know you didn't go to Catholic school, but you still go to Mass, don't you? And you're doing religion at university?

Theology, yes. And yes, I believe in God even though I wasn't educated by nuns.

And Miriam's Jewish?

Her family, yes. She sort of believes, but Miriam makes everything her own.

Including you.

Cassie laughs.

She's lucky to have you. Not that … I mean, maybe you're interested in … You know Liam thinks a lot of you, even if he is a godless tosser. His mam has never let him near a church, but he means well.

Cassie says nothing.

And me. I mean … fuck, Cassie, I'm just going to say it. I'm with the wrong sister. There, it's done. And I know you don't … I mean … Sean starts to weep quietly. I can't do this, Cassie. He lurches forward, folds to his knees, wraps his arms around her so that she is pinned to the three-legged bar stool, rests his head on her shoulder and bawls.

July 1978

The unreason of the world is more insane than any fiction.

Fire on a Taunton train kills eleven people; worst rail accident since 1967.

The world's first test-tube baby, Louise Brown, is born in Oldham.

Still at No.1, John Travolta and Olivia Newton-John continue to top the charts with 'You're the One That I Want'.

And now for the weather: The month will once again be unsettled with a depression over Iceland causing cool, wet conditions after a mild start to the month. There is a chance of thunderstorms, fog and strong, fresh winds. Sunshine will be below average.

I'm Not Supposed to Care
July 1978

Ugh, too cold. Miriam slams the window, flops onto her bed. I'm not sure pink is your colour, she adds.

Cassie looks down at the smocked pink blouse and the three-tiered cream gypsy skirt with tiny pink blossoms, a faux lace petticoat appearing round its edge. I like it. Are you coming? Cassie picks up her raffia bag. We'll miss the bus if we don't go now.

Let's stay in, Miriam says. She pushes sandals off her feet.

No.

Pardon?

I want to go. They're expecting us. Alex and Zoë have been planning this for ages and it sounds like fun.

All that sand. All that pretending to be part of the group. How is that fun, my sweet, naïve, Casilda? It isn't even a hot day.

Cassie doesn't say anything about pretence, only: I'm going. I said I would and …

You and your word, eh? It's becoming quite a thing with

you. First insisting on being part of that silly debating team, now parties on the beach and playing ridiculous games at The House. Perhaps you're outgrowing me. Miriam curls into a ball and hides her head under one arm. I'm not feeling very good, actually.

Oh, Miriam, you're fine. Put your sandals on.

Cassie, I can't come. I'm not feeling right.

Cassie had slung her bag onto a seat in the college minibus and walked back to where Miriam was standing.

I think I have an episode coming on. There's no way I can sit in that minibus all the way to Newcastle.

Cassie hovered. Someone in the minibus called her name. Joanne walked by and stopped. You ready, Cassie?

Yes, I'm just … Joanne nodded and walked towards the minibus.

Miriam?

You won't go without me, will you?

Miriam, I'm leading the team. It's the finals. We've got no chance if Luke has to step in at last minute.

Oh, well, if that's more important. I just … The judder of Miriam's arm was a breath too forceful, the way she buckled to the floor too cautious; someone not wanting to do damage on her way down, falling too carefully.

Miriam!

The movements on the ground almost convincing.

Miriam, how could you? Stop it.

Joanne and two other girls were already out of the bus. Luke hung out of the door looking helpless.

Cassie knelt down. Stop it, Miriam, she whispered.

Miriam looked up, flushed, angry. I always said you would betray me one day.

She's fine, Cassie said as the girls bent over Miriam, curled on the floor, eyes open, beginning to cry. It was just, just a near-thing. She'll be fine in a moment.

Mr Spalding appeared from the college vestibule, blanched. Cassie, is Miriam …?

She's fine. Maybe you could get someone to take her inside. She needs to rest.

Joanne and Julie returned to the bus. Mr Spalding went back inside to fetch help.

So I'm not allowed to come now?

Not unless you want me to tell them you were just faking a fit to make me stay with you. Mr Spalding isn't going to want to drive you to Newcastle if he thinks you're just coming round or might have another episode, is he?

Miriam pursed her lips and looked away.

I have to go, Miriam. He's coming back with Miss Evans. I'm sorry, really. I wanted you to be there. I have to go.

Miriam stood and turned her back.

Miriam?

Nothing.

I'll see you tomorrow.

Nothing.

Cassie phoned that evening to share the news of victory, but her mother answered. She's in bed with a terrible headache, Judith said, her voice slightly more hostile than normal. I don't think she'll be at college for the end of term.

Will you tell her we won?

I don't think I'll disturb her at the moment.

But when she …,

It was very cold of you to leave her like that when she was ill, Cassie.

The phone went dead.

The Saltburn bus is in five minutes, Miriam.

Go alone, if it's so important to you.

Please?

You're going to leave me anyway. Running off to Cambridge.

Cassie sighs. I haven't even taken the exams yet. Anyway, right now I'm going to The House.

Wait!

Miriam thrusts feet into sandals, shakes out her bell of black hair, pulls a paisley shawl from the back of a chair. Ready.

I always told everyone you'd go to Oxford, Miriam says when they are on the bus. You've defied me in that too.

I like the course at Cambridge better. You could sit entrance exams too. You'd be bound to get in.

I thought we'd go to Nottingham together.

You mean you think I'll fail the entrance exams and you'll easily get into my second choice.

Yes.

Thanks!

You're very good at Religious Education, Cassie, but it takes more than that to get into Cambridge. You can't even construct a grammatical sentence. Whatever will they make of you? And you'd have to get a whole new wardrobe, too.

Why?

You look like a gypsy.

Miriam!

Laura Ashley, that's what you need.

Who's Laura Ashley?

Heaven preserve us.

Cassie closes her eyes.

Cassie, are you falling asleep on the bus?

Sorry, no, just miles away.

Love that skirt, Zoë says, opening the door of The House.

Thanks.

You look really good in pink.

Behind her, Miriam snorts.

Could you carry a box of sandwiches down to the beach? Alex is already down there with Liam and Jeremy. I've got one cake to finish and then I'll follow you. Everyone else is going straight to the beach.

Lorraine appears, balancing cake tins. Scones, she says, grinning. We're going to feast.

Hmm, sand and processed bread, Miriam says. How delicious.

Miriam, come and help me ice the last cake, Zoë says, bustling Miriam down the narrow hallway. Sandwiches in the box there, Zoë calls over her shoulder.

Cassie picks up the cardboard box from the hall table and follows Lorraine into the street. It's cool for July and there's a bite to the breeze, but there's a long summer ahead.

Liam runs towards her from the beach as she rounds the last corner.

Let me carry that, he offers, taking the box.

Thanks.

No Miriam today?

She's helping Zoë finish a cake.

Oh. He lowers his head, hair flopping over his face. Liam deposits the box on a beach table behind a flapping windbreak. Come for a walk before everyone arrives?

Cassie glances back towards The House. Okay.

They walk in the direction of Marske, Liam putting an arm around her shoulder, trying to match his loping stride to her smaller steps. She tenses momentarily, but there is no fumbled attempt to kiss her.

When they return to the group, Miriam and Zoë have arrived with cakes. Miriam is standing next to a tall young man in black shirt and dog-collar.

I think Miri's giving Robert a hard time, Zoë says to Cassie. He's the new curate at Emmanuel Church. Plays for the opposition, but even so, you could lend him a hand. Zoë grins.

I'm just saying that the Church isn't spotless when it comes to anti-Semitism, Miriam is saying as Cassie walks over.

Cassie McManus. Cassie offers her hand.

Robert Morton, he returns, looking flushed and grateful for the intervention.

We're doing the Lyke Wake Walk next week. A group of us from Sacred Heart. You should join us — bring a party from your church — I'm sure Father Tom would love it to be ecumenical.

I'm so tired, Miriam complains.

It's only nine o'clock, Liam says before Cassie can speak. We're only just getting started.

And this game is already so tedious.

D&D, boring? Never. You just have to get into it, Liam insists, but you could always go to bed if you want. We'll look after hobbit Cassie.

Miriam scowls.

What do you think? Liam asks.

I thought I'd be an elven cleric, not a hobbit thief, Cassie says, laughing. But it's fun.

You're a great hobbit — small and quick.

Okay, you come to a room with a stone door. It doesn't appear to have any handles, Alex says.

Jeremy plots the next room on the map. Can we throw a dice to find the way in? he asks.

Maybe my hound can sniff out the route, Liam says.

Jeremy groans. Bloody dog! Can we throw a dice to kill his dog?

Shut up, Wearisome, Liam throws back.

Not this round, Alex says, grinning at Cassie. So how's your first dungeon?

Cassie nods. Fun. Shall I roll for the door handle?

Alex nods. Nice roll. Okay, the door springs open. There's an unnatural green light coming from the walls inside.

My dog goes in …

And finds itself consumed by an invisible gelatinous cube, Alex finishes.

Shit, man. You're joking?

'Fraid not.

My dog?

Dead.

Fuck. I loved that dog.

Wasn't it carrying all your gold? Jeremy asks, smiling broadly.

Eat shit, Wearisome. Let's set fire to the room, he adds, looking towards Alex.

I think I'm going to have to sleep, Miriam puts in. Cassie, could you …? Miriam pauses, looks at Cassie's expression. Never mind, I'll see you later. Come in quietly if it's late, won't you?

Cassie nods. As the door to the living room closes behind Miriam, Liam nudges Cassie and smiles.

I see your friend is joining us, Robert, the Anglican curate says stiffly as a group congregate in front of Sacred Heart, waiting for the minibuses that will take them just beyond Osmotherley to start the walk. Does she come to a lot of church events? I got the impression she was Jewish.

No, but she doesn't go to many synagogue events either. The congregation is over in Middlesbrough, Ashkenazi Orthodox.

Ah. Robert stoops as he talks and Cassie notices how uninterested he looks as she begins an effusive potted history of Ashkenazim. She also observes how eager he is to get a seat in the minibus that Miriam is not travelling in.

Shame that curate isn't in this bus, Miriam says as they set off. I have theological questions for him.

I think that might be why he's in the other bus, Cassie says.

Really? How cowardly. Or maybe he's not very certain of his faith. Or just anti-Semitic, perhaps?

Don't bait him.

I should have thought he'd want to convince me that his religion is not a death cult.

Miriam!

Miriam laughs. I think this is going to be an excellent walk.

From the Lyke Wake Stone the party set out at a moderate pace after Father Tom has led them all in prayer, first smiling at Miriam and inviting people of all faiths and none to take a quiet moment to dedicate the day to their God.

Very sensitive, Miriam whispers to Cassie.

Do you think all religions come to the same thing ultimately, then? Miriam asks Robert as soon as they are walking. Fr. Tom seems to be of a universalist persuasion. Would you agree with him?

Robert colours and stoops. Well … actually I think it's important to acknowledge Jesus as my personal Lord and saviour.

And if I don't?

Well … I … I mean Jesus stands knocking at the door … certainly in life and who's to say whether people make a final choice at death, even beyond. It's not for us to know, is it?

But no Jews in heaven, eh?

Well … I … er …

And you don't think all that crucifixion worship smacks of a death cult?

A death cult?

The slaughtered lamb, saved by blood, the punitive deity sacrificing his son, it's pretty vindictive, isn't it?

Robert stops, takes a deep breath as they labour up Carlton Bank, but can't control his rising colour. I think you're goading me, Miriam.

I think you're avoiding answering the question, Robert.

They face each other.

Look, Miriam, Cassie says softly, Roseberry Topping. I think we'll be able to see it all along the route now.

Don't try to distract me with scenery. It's a real question I'm asking this troublesome priest, Miriam replies. I know you think Christianity is all about love and peace, Casilda, setting the prisoners free, but its history is Crusades, Nazi collusion with genocide — I'm trying to find out why a messianic Jewish splinter group became an imperialist, warmongering power. Miriam turns back to Robert. Cassie here is a saint, an innocent, but you're a representative of the hierarchy. That's where we get the word for priest, isn't it? From the Greek 'hierarch'?

Isn't there plenty of sacrifice in the Old Testament? Robert asks.

We prefer not to call it that, Miriam corrects, seeing as we don't think there's a New Testament. Anyway, sacrifice went out with Amos more than seven hundred years before Christ. You must know the verses? *But let justice roll down like waters, and righteousness like an ever-flowing stream. Did you bring to me sacrifices and offerings the forty years in the wilderness, O house of Israel?* Even Abraham didn't have to sacrifice his own son in the end. God provided an alternative.

Cassie thinks Robert looks like the ram caught in the thicket. She remembers feeling like that herself two years ago, on a beach in Nairn — the alternative sacrifice.

Quite, Robert rallies. And God put an end to sacrifice completely by taking all our sins on himself and sacrificing his son, Jesus. His voice is flat.

But why does he want sacrifice in the first place? And if it's the final sacrifice, why doesn't it end?

There has to be justice as well as love. Our sin has to be accounted for and Jesus took that ...

So we could all go on feeling guilty? So a new religion could spring up to conquer the world and spread more hatred? Insane! The unreason of the world is more insane than any fiction.

Miriam's voice has risen and she is pale. Cassie tenses, looking for a tiny judder, but Robert leans towards her, puts a hand on her arm.

Man's inhumanity to man is what Jesus died for, Miriam. He stands knocking at the door of your heart, too, if you would only …

Miriam looks up, flushed, her body taut. Don't you dare! Get your hand off me! Don't you dare try to convert me to your torturing god!

She begins to run along the path ahead, towards the group of walkers who have put distance between them while they paused.

Miriam! Robert lopes after her, long strides gaining fast before his foot catches on a root curling from the stony ground where rucks of mud from the latest summer storm have hidden it. He sprawls, gripping his leg, rocking and moaning. My ankle! Oh God, my ankle!

Cassie runs towards him, halts, sees bone protruding where Robert has pulled away a grey sock.

My ankle, oh … Robert begins to vomit a thin steam of mucous.

Ahead, Miriam looks round and stops, but does not walk towards them. Instead, Cassie sees the tell-tale twitch of her arm, the colour draining from her face, hears the eerie wail as Miriam crumples.

Father Tom! Cassie shouts, as the party ahead begin turning towards the commotion. Father Tom! We need an ambulance. I'm sorry, she adds as she runs past Robert, hunches over Miriam's unconscious form on the path.

August 1978

The unreason of the world is more insane than any fiction.

Gunmen open fire on an Israeli El Al airline bus in London.

After 9 weeks at No.1, 'You're the One That I Want' is finally nudged from first place by the Commodores with 'Three Times a Lady'.

And now for the weather: Fog will persist around northern coasts for the first half of the month with more thunderstorms and cool weather. There will be sunny spells from the middle of the month, but rain will spread in late August.

I Want to Hear It From You
August 1978

Alex holds out the phone, shrugs in response to Cassie's mouthed question, disappears back into the living room. She waits for the sound of 'Any Major Dude Will Tell You' to rise before pulling the receiver close. The crying begins as she says hello.

Mandy?

Cassie closes her eyes. Mandy? What's wrong? Is it Sean?

He told me everything.

Where are you, Mandy?

Everything.

Everything about what?

Don't you dare! And at my wedding!

Cassie breathes in. Where are you, Mandy? Is Sean drunk?

Yes, yes, of course he's drunk, but he's telling the truth. I believe him.

How do you know?

It just came out, he didn't mean … And he got fired. Mandy chokes on her sobs, gulps. You're disgusting.

Miriam edges round the door, walks towards her as 'Barrytown' begins to play.

My own sister shagging my husband. You're disgusting, Catherine McManus. Really disgusting.

Cassie watches Miriam hear.

And at my bloody wedding …

Miriam's hand lands hard across the left side of her face, jolting the receiver out of earshot.

Miriam!

Miriam turns, slams the living room door.

Cassie jams the receiver into its cradle, steps forward, pauses. Miriam will be pouring out the story of betrayal regardless of its fabrication. Cassie imagines Lorraine's gloating smile, Zoë and Alex's disappointed questions, tying to understand, trying to elicit a confession; she pictures freaky Frank getting off on the thought of her with Sean. And Liam. What will Liam think?

She puts her ear against the door. Crying — faint, choked.

Then Lorraine's voice. Don't upset yourself, Miri, she's not worth having an attack over.

Cassie backs away, remembers her duffle bag is upstairs in the spare room, edges past the living room door, cautiously trying to remember where the creaks come. She's half way up the staircase when the doorbell startles her. Alex appears, casts her a sad look, shakes his head, the bell ringing constantly.

I need to speak to Cassie. Where's Cassie? Sean's speech slurs, he topples against Alex as the door opens, staggers to the stairs, kneeling.

Cassie! He waves a badly wrapped present in the air as he speaks, no doubt another Gordon Lightfoot LP. I'll take you to Ireland, Cassie, I'll … He begins to vomit as Alex hauls him to his feet.

Shit. Shit, man!

Sean heaves again. Cassie closes her eyes against the faces peering from the living room. Sean subsides.

Go and get changed, Alex. Zoë comes forward. I'll deal with this. Bring him some clean clothes too.

She pulls Sean towards the downstairs bathroom and Lorraine steps forward.

I hope you're satisfied, Cassie McManus. She slams the living room door. Alex shrugs as he passes Cassie on the stairs. She sits, staring at the pool of muddy vomit, half stands when Zoë re-appears with mop and bucket, but Zoë gestures her to sit down. When Alex passes with an armful of old clothes, Cassie makes herself small. He pauses at the bottom of the stairs, hands up the gift.

I think this is for you. Happy birthday.

Sean eventually emerges from the bathroom, dressed in clothes that hang off him, declaring his undying love, and is man-handled to the door, Tim and Liam emerging to help Alex. Ignoring the thuds against solid wood, Alex reaches up and takes the battery out of the doorbell.

Are you okay?

Cassie meets Liam's eye. He has a way of biting his lip. His eyes are grey, so much softer than his cousin's.

Cassie nods.

He's always been a piss artist. Don't worry about him. Liam shakes his head, pauses, opens his mouth, closes it again. You and him, you …

No.

Good. Liam's colour has risen. So you and Miriam …

I don't know. Is she okay?

She seems pretty upset, but she hasn't had an attack or anything.

The silence grows. Zoë re-appears in the hallway.

Why don't you go in the kitchen and make a drink for you and Miriam? I'll send her through.

Cassie nods. She would rather go and lie on Zoë and Alex's mattress in the attic amongst the rugs, shawls, incense.

In the shambolic kitchen Cassie busies herself with kettle and mugs. Miriam will notice her clumsiness; she tells herself to calm down, overfills the mugs so that tea floods the kitchen surface as Miriam walks in, dark eyes red rimmed, pale skin puffy.

Do you want sugar?

Miriam nods. She only takes sugar when she is upset. Cassie stirs too vigorously, more spills.

Good grief, Cassie, look at the mess.

Sorry.

What for?

Cassie picks up a mug, buries her face in it.

Lorraine thinks I shouldn't speak to you. Was it good?

What?

Sean. Was it good?

I wouldn't know.

Liar. Tell me. Miriam catches her breath, there is a tremor in her right arm.

Cassie steps forward. Are you okay?

I'm fine. Miriam crosses her arms, steps back. But if I do have an episode it'll be down to you. Tell me the truth.

I already did.

More tea washes over the crowded kitchen surface as Miriam slams down her mug, leaves the room.

Cassie subsides onto a painted wooden chair, chokes back the urge to cry. She scans the kitchen, begins collecting mugs of half drunk tea and coffee, used cereal bowls, crumb-strewn plates, tipping leftovers down the sink before she turns on the hot tap. She fills the bowl with water so hot she can barely touch it, heaves it onto the draining board, fills the sink, plunges her hands into the scalding soapy mess of dirty crockery, washes fast; jerky movements, tosses each clean item into the plastic bowl. When she's finished she begins scouring surfaces, looks for the sweeping brush, attacks the floor.

Wow. Frank leans on the doorjamb, lop-sided grin, too many yellow, crooked teeth. He wears the same oversized green sweater whatever the temperature. Can't remember when I last saw this place so clean.

Probably last time Zoë did it.

Frank nods. Yeah. I was worried about you, he continues. I told them we should hear you out. Maybe you need more than Miriam. It's only natural.

Cassie steps back as Frank moves forward, but his stride is longer, it's a small kitchen, the narrow junk shop table taking up the back wall beyond the strip of cracked melamine work surface. Frank reaches out a hand. You know I'm here for you.

She hunches into herself, shakes off Frank's hand. I'm fine. Me and Miriam we're, we'll be ...

Cassie can smell Frank's breath, the same sour that leaks from his sweater, the same tang that coats the moist hand brushing her face.

We could go upstairs if you like. It's your birthday.

Cassie pushes. He has her pressed against the bit of wall between the table and the door to the yard. He stoops towards her, but she twists so that his lips meet only thick hair.

Come on, Cassie. A birthday kiss at least. Her spine slams into the overhang of the windowsill.

Christ, Liam! That hurt. It was just a bit of fun.

Frank limps from the kitchen muttering.

Quite a birthday, eh?

Thank you.

You were telling the truth?

Cassie nods.

They're planning your spanking in there. Liam nods towards the living room. Metaphorically, that is. Lorraine's working Miriam up. I'm ducking out for a bit.

Cassie retreats back to the wobbly blue chair, rests her head on the table, looks up at the yard, full of soggy debris after an unseasonal downpour, the heavy winds of the Jubilee weekend have blown squalls ahead of them; a freak of low pressure. It will pass quickly, the weather forecast promised, but it has rained all day so far. She should recover her duffle bag, go home. There's going to be no beach party. She scrapes back the chair, but Lorraine is at the kitchen door.

Miriam should have slapped you harder.

I'm going home.

Lorraine holds on to both sides of the doorframe. You don't deserve Miriam. And she's a sick girl. She doesn't need scum like you. Lorraine moves aside.

When Cassie reaches the landing she hears the phone ring. I think Cassie already left for home, Mrs McManus, she hears Alex say. She drops onto the landing, back against the balustrade. Going home is a stupid idea. She shuffles into the chaotic spare bedroom, double bed jammed against one wall, a single on the opposite wall, she picks up her duffle bag and stands for a moment scanning the alley and roofs of the next terrace. The sky is still grey, but the clouds are thinning. If she stays in the spare room Frank might find her. She heads for the narrow door to the attic stairs, pulls it shut behind her and creeps up to Zoë and Alex's sanctuary. Alex has built shelves against one wall that become narrower as they rise up towards the roof. The shelves are piled with books, records, incense burners, Zoë's bright enamel necklaces, the occasional gaudy jug rescued from a charity shop. On the other wall Alex has installed a makeshift desk from a run of kitchen work surface. One end is piled with his politics books, screeds of paper jammed under the pile. At the other end is a mish-mash of Zoë's beads, silver wire and tools, the little enamelling kiln stuffed into one corner.

Cassie lifts Alex's guitar from the mattress and props it carefully against the shelves. She stretches out on the soft pile of throws and cushions, breathing in sandalwood and jasmine. The skylight above her is slightly open and she listens to the gulls, pulls a turquoise blanket over herself and drifts between waking and sleep.

In her dreams she is in the tiny chapel at Wilton. Christopher's coffin stands on trestles at the front of the aisle.

Doing wheelies, Miriam had told her. He was trying to impress Marcia. He couldn't accept that she just wasn't interested.

Dead? Cassie asked again, unbelieving.

I already told you that, my innocent Casilda. It's quite a story, isn't it? Betrayal, romance, death.

It's not a story, Miriam. Christopher's dead. I only saw him two days ago. And he only just got the motorbike the day before that.

That's such a cliché, Cassie. People always say that about the dead — I just saw them. I suppose the funeral will be heaving. Do you think Marcia will be there?

After they had mumbled the twenty-third psalm (Stolen from us, Miriam hissed as it was announced) the vicar invited the congregation to sit while Christopher's school-friend said a few words. Liam had walked forward slowly, flushed and pulling on his white collar.

Christopher was the best, he said. Full of life. He flushed deeper red as Christopher's mother's soft weeping became a howl, shifted from foot to foot. He was always ready for a laugh, and a great friend, but what I wanted to do was read a poem he wrote just before … I mean … anyway:

> Because you do not love me
> life has lost its glow;
> but if you change your mind
> then you'll truly know
> that I'm sincere and kind,
> together we could find
> heaven here below.
>
> And if you will not listen
> I'll try another way
> to make you see I love you
> and will never stray …

From the edge of the last pew a girl rose and began to push through those without seats, standing at the back of the airless chapel.

You should hear this, Marcia, Liam called.

The girl turned, her eyes puffy, pale skin daubed pink.

No, I shouldn't. I didn't ask him to fall in love with me. I didn't ask him to do wheelies in front of my house and kill himself …

A hiss came from the gathered family and friends. The vicar stood, flapping arms ineffectually. The wailing mother stood and turned towards the back of the chapel.

Little hussy! she screamed. Nasty little tart. I know all about you, leading my poor boy on. Look at him. She flailed towards the coffin. Look at what you've done. She sank to the floor, bawling.

I … Marcia said, then wept, turning to leave, finding her way barred by an assortment of Christopher's friends.

Let her through!

Miriam was in the aisle.

Jew-bitch, someone hissed.

Let her through. She's right. He brought this on himself. Not every girl wants some idiot boy fawning after her. Some of us have more sense. More dignity. There's no betrayal here. Let her through!

Miriam hurled herself towards the wall of Christopher's supporters, who flinched, broke rank as Marcia ran out of the chapel and Miriam stopped, shook almost imperceptibly, collapsed, one arm twitching, an eerie wail coming from her contorted body.

Please, the vicar intoned, please remain calm, please …

It's dark when Cassie wakes. She gathers her things, pulls a crocheted shawl from her pink and blue striped duffle bag, throws it over the cheesecloth shirt, smoothes pink gypsy skirt over broderie anglaise petticoat, pulls apart her unkempt plait and combs fingers through thick fair waves. She edges down the narrow stairs from the attic, inches open the door to the landing. In the bathroom she drinks from the tap, splashes her face.

Standing outside the spare room, she hears Lorraine's voice. I know she looks like butter wouldn't melt, Miri, but she doesn't fool me. Sly. And that family. Her sister's always been a tart and there's about fifty cousins, you know. Irish mafia or something. Uncles in and out of prison. My Aunty Jean lives next door to Cassie's Aunty Sue, not much older than us, and on her second baby, different dads of course, and Aunty Jean heard that while this Sue was in hospital popping out the second, her — whatever he is, not her husband, anyway — but the bloke she's shacked up with, he was out doing another one of Cassie's aunties who lives down the street and now this other one is knocked up as well. It's like living near a pack of wild dogs, my Aunty Jean says. Cassie's mam puts on all these airs and graces like she wasn't one of them, but my mam always says the apple doesn't fall far from the tree and apparently their house is awful inside.

I can vouch for that, Cassie hears Miriam say. I never eat there. But Cassie is …

Cassie takes a deep breath. Miriam will defend her. Miriam won't believe Sean. Until death, it's all life, Cassie, Miriam had told her last summer when they finished O levels. Remember. Yes, Cassie remembers. And on the beach the year before, the sands golden white, stretching for miles, the coarse marram of the dunes, watching their footprints imprint into the wet sand near the tideline, four small neat prints: four, then four, then six. She saved Miriam. Miriam collapsed, emptied out, gone elsewhere; the man kicking her experimentally; running back, the rock, hurling it, not hard enough, hands around her throat, rough breath, white cotton tearing, falling onto sand. And then? She saved Miriam. The story won't end here.

Oh, you're so kind, Miri, Lorraine simpers. But she's still one of them, no matter how many books she reads. I mean, fancy screwing her sister's husband on their wedding day. What a cliché. You can't get much lower than that. She's just not what she seems, little miss innocent's another McManus slut when you get down to it.

Yes.

Cassie gasps, wonders if she is still standing, holds herself against the wall, slides down.

Yes, Miriam says again.

Cassie slinks towards the stairs, sits at the top, head in her lap, edges down, one step, one step, stops half way to sit again. The story and the facts no longer match.

The story and the facts … Once there was a Moorish princess, Casilda, daughter of the king of Toledo and a Berber girl, who died in childbirth, she tells herself. She had long golden hair, green eyes, pale skin. She wore only white or the palest blue, almost white like the halo of sky around the sun. My hair is fair, not golden, my eyes are grey; signs of enchantment, she tells herself, repeating what Miriam has insisted. For six years Cassie has seen only the story that Miriam has told her. Belief is her gift.

She chokes back a sob. God, this is the end of the story. I can't go on, she says out loud.

Cassie? Liam is in front of her. He kneels on the step below, wraps himself around her, rocks. He's grown tall, over a foot taller than Cassie, broad, brown eyes rich with light, dark hair that frames his face in loose curls. He holds her close, tight, rocks, kisses. You're okay, Cassie, you're okay. She feels tears, silent, streaming, doesn't hear the soft click of the door, doesn't see Lorraine and Miriam on the landing above, watching as Liam rocks her, covers her tears in kisses, lifts her, tells her all shall be well, this is the start of another story.

Part II

In the first part of this story we left the Toledan princess, Casilda, also known as Cassie McManus, and her indefatigable defender-turned-betrayer, Ben Haddaj, also known as Miriam, deep in conflict; Miriam having delivered a cruel blow that might have broken Cassie if it had not been for Liam, who was more than ready to offer comfort. And this might have been the end of the story, but I could not let that happen. After all, theirs was an extraordinary encounter; one that in another age minstrels would have sung ballads about; a romance full of adventure that should not be left unwritten.

I'm Not Saying
October 1992

In the story, there is an incident so slight, so small, so brutal that the character, Cassie, cannot go on. She overhears something that shatters her belief in Miriam and in the world they've shared. A tiny act of betrayal is all it takes for her to step outside of the spell.

And your character — Cassie — you've given her your own name. Is that significant?

The interviewer leans in.

Well, I've given her a version of my name, but the book is very much fiction. I think the name was a way of imagining myself into that persona, but of course none of this really happened. I mean my other character, Miriam, believes she is an immortal who has lived through many incarnations, but she's actually a teenager living in Teesside at the end of the 70s. I wanted to examine how a young woman like that would fare. And I was also interested in how someone else might prop up her fantasy world, even enter into it.

And is Cassie able to do that?

Yes, for a long time she is the one who really believes all this. Miriam is obsessed with a romanticised past gleaned from bits of literature. She hates the world she lives in and feels alienated. She is the outsider as the only Jewish girl in her class, the girl with epilepsy, the girl with elderly parents. She hates contemporary music. She knows, really, that Cassie is a girl from a rough family on the local council estate, but she wants to believe that she is an eleventh century Spanish princess and saint, Casilda, enchanted and trapped. The problem is that Miriam knows it's a story, that narrative can't actually replace experience, but can only register something about the quality of experience. So she is struggling to create an identity that insulates her against loneliness and ridicule. She is trying to convince herself that she is someone else, and in a world of political and social madness, her world view is perhaps not as insane as it appears — she constantly remarks that the insanity of the world is madder than any fiction, so why not invent herself? But she can only sustain this invented identity if someone else accepts it and reflects it back to her.

And that's where Cassie comes in?

Absolutely. There is a naïve quality and pliancy to Cassie, despite her intelligence, that allows her to believe all this.

Belief is her gift?

Yes, that's a motif running through the novel. Cassie trusts that the story and the facts can be the same, but once she is betrayed by Miriam, her certainty unravels.

And that leads to …?

Catherine laughs.

Well, that would be telling. People have to read the book to find out what happens in the end.

Quite so.

Eric Johns swivels his chair towards the studio audience.

I've been talking to Catherine McManus, author of *This is the End of the Story*.

He turns back.

Catherine, thank you for being with us this evening and all the best with your book.

Kitty!

Catherine halts. It's dark outside the studio, rain fogging the air.

Kitty!

He is closer now, half way over the road, out of the shelter of the doorway opposite, a tall, dishevelled figure with a smile that has always looked sarcastic.

I was in the studio, he says. I wanted to see you. You do realise all this isn't right, don't you? I've read the book. It's …

It's fiction, Liam.

Like hell, it is! It's awful. For God's sake, Kitty …

Catherine. My name is Catherine and I'm getting drenched. I …

We could go to a café.

Liam reaches out to take her arm, but she avoids his touch.

No.

You owe me …

No, Liam, I don't.

Catherine begins walking towards the tube station at the end of the road. He lopes after her.

Bloody awful. Did you have to make me look like that?

Catherine stops. I'm going this way. You are going somewhere else. Goodbye, Liam.

Heartless, bitch. Cold, you were always bloody cold.

His voice pursues her as she descends underground, but he doesn't follow her. In the tunnel, she pauses, leans against a wall. Tears stab, but she clamps her jaw, clenches her eyes closed for a moment, begins to walk, briskly, towards her train.

Let me help, Catherine says as the man ahead of her on the office stairs drops a sheath of manuscript pages.

He frowns. Thank you, he says. I'm here to meet someone about this. He gestures towards the tumble of pages. Good start to getting published, he quips, scrabbling after the paper.

She smiles. I'm Catherine, by the way, she says, scooping up pages. Catherine Anne McManus.

His frown deepens. Simon Garrett, he says. Here to meet Catherine Anne McManus. Have I blown it already?

Catherine thinks how blue his eyes are, hopes that she will

like his writing.

It's a family name, she tells him over coffee in the meeting room. My family still call me Cassie. Probably someone was short tongued four generations back, my mam says — Cathy became Cassie. I don't know. There's at least one in every generation of our family anyway — my aunt is Catherine Anne, my nanna, great-gran — all called Cassie. I always wanted to be called Kat when I was little, not Cassie. And then I was Kitty for a while, but I won't go into that. And now it's Catherine.

She doesn't mention being Casilda.

In the little third floor flat, she throws open the window, looks across the roofs of the old town towards the ocean. She has always loved the sea. She will sleep with the windows open behind the green shutters so that she can hear the sea in her dreams. It's mild here, October in Nice.

She cannot not stop the memories, much fingered as they are.

Trust me, Cassie, you'll get your island.

My island?

Metaphorically, dear Casilda. You'll go to Oxford and succeed in everything you do and live happily ever after. Ben Haddaj will have finally saved you.

Cambridge. I'd corrected her. And I haven't got in yet.

You will. You've been trained by the best.

My island became a recurring dream, an island no one had ever stepped on, but there it was …

Miniature, mist-shrugged, magnetic. From the shore, shushing waves lapping shale, stepping stones slick-slippery standing proud of the water, lifting first one foot, then the next, slowly making towards an island that seemed to grow larger, fog furling its hidden heart so that the view was only of its ragged edge, gnawed granite, split slate giving to tussocky marsh, moss-mottled; an island no one had ever stepped on, and one that no one would leave. Wind whittled at the water, carved waves that soaked stepping stones, the last one submerged, then the one behind that; stretched to the next as another drowned, harried on to an island no one had ever stepped on before; an island that no one would leave …

What really happened was that I got my island — I got into Cambridge, then found a job in publishing, first with a theological press, later with a literary agency, and, of course, marriage to Liam; I got my island and I couldn't escape it …

She got bronchitis in her first term at university and he drove her back to Teesside.

Oh, God, Liam, it's …

She glanced around the ground floor flat, an almost empty, bare-walled living room furnished with two sagging floor cushions and an ancient TV on an upturned tea-chest. She shuffled towards the bedroom, clutching her chest as she coughed and flopped onto a creaking bed. Tea-chests stood either side of it and old suitcases against the wall masqueraded as cupboards.

It's freezing in here.

Middlesbrough rain pelted the window, greyer than the net curtains pinned to the frame.

Liam nodded. I've got an extra blanket somewhere. You'll soon warm up.

I didn't really know what to get, Liam mumbled, passing her a present, the wrapping paper already torn at the corners.

Thank you.

She pulled off the thin paper and held the record uncertainly.

You don't like it, do you?

I … I don't know. I'm not sure I've heard any Bob Marley.

You could pretend to look interested.

I am … I …

She rose and fumbled with the record player that sat on the floor by the television. Listened. It's … got a nice beat. What's skanking?

For fuck's sake, Kitty.

I don't think you should move to Cambridge, she ventured in bed, huddled deep beneath the blankets.

What?

I think it's a mistake. I think all of it's a mistake. Maybe we should …

What the fuck are you saying? I've just given up a good job to follow you to bloody Cambridge and now you tell me it's all a mistake! What am I supposed to do now?

I thought ICI needed electricians. They'd take you back, you said yourself they offered you more money when you said you were leaving …

Fucking hell! Liam held her neck tight against the mattress. You ridiculous little bitch. One lousy Christmas day and you're through with me.

He shook her slightly, let go, ignored the coughing.

Go to sleep and don't be so bloody stupid.

It's like there's this other Kitty, the college chaplain told her. Someone on the verge of making an entrance, who hasn't quite got the confidence to break out. When she does, I think she'll be really interesting.

She worked harder to cage that person away, imagined she was hiding her slow break-down. There were days when she was terrified of being alone; days when she told him to leave. He sneered at the ridiculousness of her.

You're always writing essays or in that bloody chapel, Liam complained. If you join the debating thing or some amateur dramatics crowd, what am I supposed to do? Anyway, I hate all that — you know I do. If you need another bloody hobby, find something less aggressive.

She found a jazz ballet class that met in the daytime while Liam was at work. She did not have to speak at a dance class.

At Christmas she bought presents for him to give to her, wrapped and labelled them, thanked him.

She found a 1920s dress in a shop in Covent Garden, blousy red flowers on blue chiffon, wore it to her twenty-first birthday party after finals. He got drunk and spoke only in double-entrendres. She danced with friends, with the college chaplain, smiled all evening, cried herself to sleep, careful not to wake him.

In Bristol she danced at a studio at the bottom of Jacob Well's Road, took out a subscription to *Spare Rib*, began wearing only purple, adopted a blue-eyed white cat.

On the day she was offered her first job in publishing they drove to Castle Coch, wandered around the folly grounds. She wore silver earrings, each with a stained glass fairy-tale castle in the centre. They camped in the Forest of Dean, read *The Dark is Rising* aloud in the tent by torchlight. He was pleased about the job, keen to move to London. The summer stretched before them and she fell asleep not thinking of their overdraft or arguments.

In his second year at poly Liam decided that media studies was rubbish. His tutor hated him and everyone in the department was stupid. She believed him; belief was her gift, after all. He befriended a girl even thinner than her.

I invited Lisa for dinner again on Friday, Liam told her. She needs feeding up.

You do know she's in love with you?

Rubbish. She's just lonely. She's into animal rights and doesn't mix much. So you're jealous of her, eh?

No, but she thinks you're interested. It's not very kind.

Lisa got ill after breaking into a laboratory to release animals used in medical research.

They can't find out what's wrong with her. I thought she should maybe stay with us for a bit. She can't look after herself.

No.

Don't be so bloody heartless, Kitty. Anyway, I already told her it's okay. She tried to kill herself before, I'm worried about her. Lisa's sick and suicidal. She needs me, unlike some people I could mention.

At Christmas she bought presents from him to give to her, mostly text-books for the part-time PhD she'd started. She wrapped and labelled them herself, thanked him.

She looked out of the window at the Boxing Day snow.

Did I mention Lisa's coming for lunch?

What? I thought she'd dropped out?

She has, but she's working in this awful family business and really depressed. Oh, and don't forget she's vegan …

No.

What do you mean?

Cook for her yourself.

She spent the afternoon on a bench in Greenwich Park,

shivering in the snow, reading *Texts of Terror*, uncertain whether her tears were for Jephthah's daughter or herself.

Sometimes she told him she wanted to leave, but he always retorted that she was being ridiculous. When she stopped getting up in the mornings, he drove her to her mother's house in Redcar.

I want a divorce, she told him.

You don't know what you want, he replied.

They returned to Redcar after Liam's finals, travelling for Jeremy's wedding, Liam grouching about 'Wearisome' getting married in a 'bloody Catholic church'. Dropping her off at The House, where Zoë and Alex were also staying, Liam backed the car into the gate before she was through it. She beat on the reversing vehicle, squeezed between car and wrought iron.

The baby stopped moving.

Nothing I can do, the locum GP told Zoë. Call me when she starts to lose it.

It was Zoë and Alex who took her to hospital. She felt a clot slip between her legs, blood thick, gelatinous, oozing through layers of clothing, the blanket they'd wrapped her in. She thought of Casilda's Berber mother, haemorrhaging after giving birth to her fragile daughter, and, later, Casilda bleeding without respite.

Jeremy found Liam with Lorraine, told him the news.

She went to bed on a hot day in June, 1988, slept all day, all night, woke exhausted, slept through another year, most of it spent with her mother in Redcar before they found the tiny cottage in Wales.

The last time she saw Miriam …

'… to write,' de Beauvoir said in *The Prime of Life*, 'something has to go adrift in life, we have to no longer be able to take reality for granted.'

What really happened was that when I came home, overwhelmed by all that Miriam had denied, I slept and slept. When I woke I was sufficiently adrift to write what really happened; adrift enough to say nothing to Liam, except: 'This is the end of the story. Leave.'

In the little flat in Nice, she throws open the window, looks across the roofs of the old town towards the ocean. She has always loved the sea. She will sleep with the windows open behind the green shutters so that she can hear the sea in her dreams.

For Lovin' Me
December 1978

Once there was a Moorish princess, Casilda, daughter of the king of Toledo and a Berber princess, who died in childbirth. She had long golden hair, green eyes, pale skin. She wore only white or the palest blue, almost white like the halo of sky around the sun.

None of this really happened.

My plaits were coarse and fair, not golden, my eyes grey; signs of enchantment, Miriam insisted, and I went along with her because I felt sorry for her. She had no friends and everyone was mean to her. Well, Joanne and a few others treated her okay, but they would never have invited her to a party unless she came with me.

I wanted her to feel like someone cared. She had those awful fits and her mum was weird and snobby. I was being kind.

We were never a couple. Just best friends. But she took it all too far. She always took everything too far.

I don't know what happened on the beach. There was a man. Miriam had a fit. There was a family who helped us get back to the caravan. Sometimes I dream about that day. There is always a white skirt, ripped, then nothing. My diaries are no help. It was only three years ago, but it's like reading something written by an alien.

There are footprints in the sand. The singing sand. Song-crunched. Sand rubbing sand, grain by grain, into song; the world in a grain of sand, sand singing. Footprints running beside ours. Our footprints are small: small and narrow, small and wide. Bare footprints — heel to toe. Sandalled footprints — compact, toeless. Two sets of footprints, then three. Did he come from behind? Silent. Did he come from the forest? We would have seen him approach. From the sea? He was dry. Tall, dry, dressed in swimming trunks. Blue. Red? Blue or red or? Blue, definitely blue. Blue sea or grey or green? The sea isn't blue, really, is it? Grey-green. White foam. Scum coloured? Yellow-grey. The sand was golden. The sand was white? The sand was … the sand was singing. There were three sets of footprints washed away by sea, by foam. Spume. And rocks. The beach was a long ribbon of sand, white-gold and singing, no rocks. Miriam picked up a rock. Or I picked up a rock. There was the wailing sound that Miriam makes before her eyes turn inward, before she is not there. There was the way her arm judders. Nothing happened. Miriam had a fit and a family helped us back to the caravan. And in the night I heard Judith crying, Mr Jacobs pacing the caravan. I heard a roar, Mr Jacobs who hardly spoke, roared. Or I dreamt a roar, dreamt I heard weeping, woke up and Miriam was there. And nothing had happened.

I never believed the stories. We played games. It was a way for Miriam to feel important. She had this notion that she would teach me about narrative and how reality works. Miriam always said that in a mad world, no fiction can ever be thought of as insane. You only have to pick up a newspaper to see that. I wrote an essay for my Cambridge entrance exams: 'Narrative cannot order experience, but only register something about the quality of experience. Discuss.' Miriam knew that. I knew it too, of course I did, but she needed me to pretend I didn't know it so that I could order experience for her. I didn't believe it, but if

I'd said that to her, she would have been left in a chaotic world that made no sense. Neither of us believed that I was Casilda in a former life, or that she was Ben Haddaj, or that we had once been Leonidas and Gorgo in ancient Sparta, but we acted out the stories, because she needed it. I never believed, not really.

I wasn't the one who broke the spell.

It was the worst birthday I've ever had. I can still hear Lorraine's voice, relishing the spite:

I mean, fancy screwing her sister's husband on their wedding day of all days. What a cliché. You don't get much lower than that, Miriam. She's just not what she seems, little miss innocent's another McManus slut when you get down to it.

Not that I cared what Lorraine thought of me. It would have been worse if Alex and Zoë had believed all that hysteria Mandy caused, but Lorraine always enjoyed the misery of others. And it's hardly like she proved much of a friend to Miriam either. It was an awful thing to hear, but it was what Miriam said that undid everything.

Yes.

That's all she said — *Yes*. Twice. She said it twice. It wasn't a mistake or something she wanted to take back. *Yes.*

Miriam always said I would betray her. But it wasn't that way round in. And all I could do was write in my journal.

The story and the facts. Stories are made up. Tales we tell to make the world safe; trying to line the hard cave we live in with soft fabrics: the lies we tell ourselves:

there are no monsters, once upon a time, there was a Moorish princess, Casilda …

Facts like iron splinters falling as rain. The winter of discontent. Almost tripped into a manhole during a power cut while I was walking home. The Yorkshire Ripper. Idi Amin. Facts insane as caged wild dogs. Less than ten years ago epileptics couldn't legally marry. In 1190 the Jews in York were burnt alive in Clifford's Tower or murdered, all those who hadn't already committed suicide in terror. The Holocaust less than forty years ago. Facts. The story is the least insanity. But I wanted the story and the facts to match, thought they had to match. They don't. But I could make myself believe. Belief is my gift. No — belief used to be my gift. Don't believe. Yes, was all Miriam said. Assent loud as hell breaking open. Yes. Yes. And now I don't believe. Never believed. Belief is pretence. Kierkegaard says if we act as if we have faith, then faith will come. I acted and acted and … the story and the facts don't match. Don't believe. This is the end of the story. This is the end.

Yes.

I saw you on the stairs. With him. She said it like I was the one who had betrayed her, but that's not how it was. The story and the facts never matched, did they? There are monsters. Once there was someone called Casilda and we know hardly anything about her and I wasn't Casilda in a former life and Ben Haddaj has not followed me through centuries waiting to save me. No one can save me. There are stories. There are facts. They're all insane.

Perhaps I should stop keeping journals.

Once there was a Moorish princess, Casilda, daughter of the king of Toledo and a Berber girl who died in childbirth. She had long golden hair, green eyes, pale skin. She wore only white or the palest blue, almost white like the halo of sky around the sun.

None of this really happened.

What really happened was that Liam was there and he held me and rocked me and said everything would be alright; made me feel safe again.

Liam kissed her tears, reached up, stroked away the damp patches. Come on.

Cassie looked confused, shook her head. Miriam's in the spare room with Lorraine.

He smiled. No, come downstairs. I was thinking I could make you a drink. Or we could go to the pub if you like.

Would they serve us?

Not you. He grinned. You look about 14, but we don't have to get alcohol. Or we could just walk for a bit, call in at Maynard's and buy a chocolate orange. Whatever you like.

I like those candied ones, Cassie had said.

Yeah? Candied orange it is then. He stood up and pulled her after him.

On the beach he wound his arm around her as they walked, fed her slices of chocolate orange.

Sorry about getting the wrong sort, he said, grinning, those candied ones are too much like real fruit for my taste, though.

They walked all the way to Marske, came off the beach near *The Ship Inn* and into the town to wait for a bus.

Meet you tomorrow, he said. Near Pacitto's?

What really happened was that I did my Cambridge entrance exams wearing Liam's embroidered blue shirt for luck, my little framed picture of the Virgin Mary on the desk in front of me. Miriam managed to wish me good luck, but she didn't take the exams herself. We'd been polite all term, still sat together in English, but I hadn't been to her house since August.

Not far to my house, he said. I'll make some Nescafé. Might even have some biccies in.

Cambridge, eh? Liam asked, handing her a steaming mug. So you won't be staying around here for long.

Well, I'm not there yet, but I'll go to university somewhere. Nottingham was my second choice. They've offered me three Cs, which is a doddle, but it's where Miriam is going so I hope I do get into Cambridge.

Never liked that girl, Liam said. So you don't fancy Teesside Poly?

You're joking.

Suppose so. Just seems sad you going away when we've just got together.

We can still …

Yeah, my last girlfriend moved to Derby. Soon found someone else. And all those nobs at Cambridge. Don't stand a chance, do I? What are your other choices then, if the local's no good?

Nottingham, Newcastle, Lancaster and Aberystwyth.

Yeah? Newcastle's not so far. Yeah, we could manage Newcastle. You really going to put yourself through extra exams just to go to some swanky place full of nobs?

It would be amazing to get in.

Sounds awful to me. Newcastle's more like here. You'd fit in better there. Fancy going for a Chinese on Friday, by the way? My mate Chris is going with his girlfriend, asked if we wanted to come along.

Great. I've never been to a Chinese restaurant before and I'll have done my last entrance exam on Friday.

If you're sure you want to do them.

Yes. Nearly time for my bus.

Liam knocked the cup of cold instant coffee over as he stood. Shit! Oh Christ, sorry, Cassie.

Cassie dabbed at brown stains on her white blouse.

Have I ruined it? Shit.

It'll wash. Well, it might. I'm more worried about getting the bus home looking like this at the moment.

Right. Liam paused. I'll get you a shirt. I've got this embroidered one my mam got me. I hardly ever wear it. It's a bit small as well.

He returned with a tea towel to mop up the spilled coffee and a turquoise shirt covered in fine white thread.

This Saturday, Liam called through the bathroom door while Cassie peeled off her wet blouse. Thought we'd go and see *Death on the Nile* before it finishes.

Cassie emerged with the shirt half tucked into jeans, its too-long sleeves rolled up.

I've got the debate this weekend; it's the regional final.

Liam scrunched his face. You don't want me to go to that, do you? One of those was enough for me — this house is totally up itself. And I hate the way you argue — makes you seem so aggressive. Freaks me out.

What really happened was that I got into Cambridge and Liam was amazing about it and Miriam couldn't stand to think I could exist without her.

Sitting at the back of the history class, Cassie was composing lines of poetry in a notebook when Mr Spalding entered and placed a hand on her shoulder.

I'd just like to borrow Cassie for a moment, Mr Spalding said as Mr Forrest looked up from his well-used notes on Oliver Cromwell, currently being read to the class.

Mr Forrest nodded. Yes, of course.

Just had a phone call, Cassie, exciting news, but can't say any more till we get to Miss Doone's office or she'll have my guts. Mr Spalding grinned and Cassie trotted to keep up with his loping pace.

Well, Catherine, Miss Doone said as they came through the office door. You really do have a lot more going on than you let show sometimes.

She waved a piece of paper: An exhibition, Catherine. Well

done.

A what?

You've passed, Catherine, better than passed. An exhibition is a small bursary from your chosen college, given to those who perform particularly well in the entrance exams — there are scholars and exhibitioners and you are an exhibitioner. Congratulations, Catherine. Would you like to phone home?

Home? Oh … I think … I'll tell them in person, but thank you. Wow. I've really got in?

Indeed.

Wow. Cassie sat in a padded office chair in front of Miss Doone's desk. I feel a bit dizzy. She shook herself slightly. But good — thank you. Thank you. Does Mr Hopkins know?

Not yet, but I'm sure he wouldn't mind being interrupted. He's teaching lower sixth in the RE room at the moment.

Thank you. Yes. I'll go tell him. Thank you.

Cassie skipped up the hallway. At the corner of the corridor she did a small pirouette, ran up the stairs.

Back in the history room, Mr Forrest was almost as excited as Mr Hopkins had been, even if Cassie wasn't going to be reading history as he'd hoped, but theology. At the bell, classmates crowded round to congratulate her, Miriam hanging back to the end.

I knew you'd do it, Cassie, Miriam said when the crowd had dispersed. You should come for Sunday lunch this weekend. The elderly parents will be thrilled. And you really should look into a Laura Ashley dress or two when you get to Cambridge — you'd look adorable. She paused. So — I'm going to Nottingham alone then? Miriam smiled weakly.

I wish you'd done the exams.

Oh, I'm not as extraordinary as you think, Cassie. Strange, but not extraordinary.

Oh, Miriam, you're …

Miriam waved a hand, put a finger over Cassie's lips. Didn't I always tell you that you'd get your island?

Cassie smiled. I don't think I'll make governor of Cambridge. And I know you only meant metaphorically, she added before Miriam could correct her.

Yes, Miriam agreed. I hope Liam will be pleased for you too.

Oh, he will.

Lunch on Sunday, then?

Yes. Thank you. And afterwards we'll go to The House?

Definitely. My dad will give us a lift to Saltburn and we can tell The Gang your amazing news.

The band playing in the pub was called The Crabs. The music was loud, competing with voices that screamed in monotone. Cassie hugged her glass of lemonade. Liam gulped down Old Peculiar.

So you're really going? he asked, again.

Of course. It's Cambridge, I'm hardly going to turn them down, am I?

Newcastle's a pretty good university, isn't it? Even Nottingham? Though you're better off without freaky Miriam, that's for sure.

Yes, they're both good — but they're not Cambridge.

Suppose we'll have to get married then.

What?

If you go without me I won't stand a chance, will I? We should at least get engaged.

Is that a proposal?

What if it was?

Pardon?

What would you say if I asked you to marry me?

I suppose … I mean … yes … I …

That's settled then. Let's go for Sunday lunch in the country somewhere. *The Lion* on Blakey Ridge. Then we can tell The Gang in the evening.

Oh … I promised Miriam …

Shit. That girl gets where a draft wouldn't. We just got engaged and you're having lunch with her instead of me?

It's not like that, Liam. It's just … I haven't been to her house in months and her mam and dad have done a lot for me and …

Oh, fine. We'll go another time. Anyway, I have to get going. Said I'd meet Chris and Fran at the folk club tonight.

No way, man, Terry said.

For a start, all marriage is ownership, Alex added.

Yeah, Zoë confirmed. Really oppressive shit, Liam.

And for a second thing, your motives are totally suspect, man. I mean no way would you have asked her to marry you if she wasn't going to university. You're just shit scared, and you're trying to keep her down. And she's seventeen for fuck's sake.

Yeah, and jury's out on whether she's even into blokes, Zoë put in. Her and Miriam had a sweet thing there for ages.

That was kid's stuff, Liam countered. They were never … it wasn't … you know — and why shouldn't I be scared of losing her?

Come on, Jeremy added, you can't stand her having any space at all. You don't like her having Miriam as a friend. You don't like her going to church. You don't like her leading the debate team. She's given up the amateur dramatics group since you got together. You're keeping her down, and now you're going to follow her to Cambridge and shadow her every move. It's pathetic.

Fuck off, Wearisome. Why shouldn't I have an opinion on her friends, especially when they're freaky? Miriam just manipulates Cassie —

Oh and you don't? That's rich! Jeremy's voice was raised.

Shh, Zoë cautioned. We don't want to wake Cassie.

Sorry, Jeremy said, turning back to Liam. You're a right hypocrite. Cassie has a chance to make something of her life and you'll drag her down.

Eat shit. And I've never made Cassie stop debating …

Only cos she didn't let you, Jeremy contended.

And as for the church, Liam cut in. I've always hated the Catholic church. It's evil. Telling people how to live, stopping contraception, colluding with the Nazis.

Broken bloody record, Jeremy said.

On the staircase, Cassie ducked behind the banister as Jeremy slammed the living room door behind him and headed into the kitchen.

We're just saying, Alex said, his voice only just audible, that this is serious shit, Liam. I mean if two people realise that marriage is just state ownership and fraught with all kinds of misogyny and slavery, but they go ahead against all the odds because they're mad optimists with their eyes wide open, then good luck to them. But we just don't think that's the case here and —

I'm going to bed, Liam said. You can spare me the rest of the speech.

Cassie scurried towards the bedroom before Liam could discover her on the stairs.

Ribbon of Darkness
February 1979

Miriam must have heard all about The Gang trying to talk Liam out of getting engaged to me, probably from Terry. He used to give her lifts home when I stayed over at The House and I think he was quietly in love with her. I think Miriam knew it. She made remarks about Teesside Poly being a backwater for people who couldn't get into real universities, so Terry never said anything to her.

Miriam liked the idea that Alex and Zoë thought we shouldn't get married. She felt vindicated, so even when I told her I was still going to get engaged to Liam, Miriam was friendly again. It wasn't the same as it had been at school. She stopped calling me Casilda, but she invited me to hear her singing in Handel's Messiah at the big Anglican Church round the corner from The House, just before Christmas. She said all the messianic stuff was Jewish anyway, Christians had just misappropriated it, and the music was good so why shouldn't she sing in it.

And, in the New Year, when Zoë said The House should throw a party for Miriam's eighteenth birthday, Miriam was thrilled.

Do you think Tim will be there?

Lorraine's Tim?

She doesn't own him, Cassie. They're not even engaged.

They've been going out for ages, haven't they?

He's going to Oxford, Miriam said, ignoring the question. He did seventh term entrance, so not as brilliant as you, doing it fourth term, but still pretty bright. And history too — I like that.

Sorry, Miriam — are you saying you're interested in Tim because he's going to Oxford?

Lorraine will be lucky to get into a poly. It's not like he'll stay with her.

I'll find you another blouse to put on, Zoë offered. She scowled at Liam. Go and sit down, klutz.

Liam smirked and ambled into the sitting room.

Cassie held the beer-stained top away from her body. It was just an accident, she said, remembering the shirt he'd spilled cold coffee on just before her Cambridge entrance exams.

Zoë nodded and they headed for the attic room.

I love it in here.

Zoë smiled. Yeah, though if Alex gets his way, we'll be living on a barge by the summer.

Don't you want to?

I don't mind really. I'd probably make better sales of the

jewellery if we were taking tourists on boats. And living with Frank can get wearing. I've just got used to this little sanctuary, I suppose.

Zoë rifled through a drawer and held out a cheesecloth shirt.

Thanks.

By the autumn there won't be many of us left anyway. Lorraine's off to Manchester, Tim to Oxford, you and Miriam will be going to university. Terry's applying for teacher training in the midlands somewhere. Maybe it's time for a change.

Yes. Cassie froze …

That noise …

Cassie was leaving the room before Zoë could finish the sentence.

Miriam!

She almost missed the top step of the stairs from the attic as she scuttled down, Zoë close behind her.

At the entrance to the kitchen Miriam laid still, her eyes vacant.

My God! Lorraine's face drained from flushed to pallid. That's not even human.

Cassie knelt by Miriam.

I didn't even touch her, Lorraine said.

Cassie turned abruptly. What? What do you mean, you

didn't touch her?

I just wanted to warn her off, is all. Sending bloody love letters to my boyfriend. Who the fuck does she —

Shut up, Cassie snapped.

Shall I call someone? An ambulance? Zoë crouched beside Cassie and Miriam.

She's probably putting it on. Liam stood in the doorway to the living room, his words slurred. She's always doing it.

Shut up, Cassie said louder. Yes — can you call an ambulance, Zoë?

Judith sits by Miriam's bed and smiles wanly when Cassie enters the hospital room each day.

Cassie sits on the edge of the second chair.

No change, Judith says each day.

Cassie nods.

She doesn't stay for long. Mr Jacobs will be here from work soon and only two visitors are allowed.

She leaves a few minutes later, passing Mr Jacobs in the long green corridor.

No change, she whispers as they pass one another, and he nods.

She pictures Miriam asleep; olive skin, hair a tangle of soot and pitch. They have known so many defeats, but Miriam chose her and together they have braved the world. How many times had she warned Miriam not to go looking for trouble? Let's find another road, she would always say. But she hadn't seen trouble coming that day.

God, this is the end of the story. I can't go on, she says to the empty street.

The curtain is pulled around Miriam's bed. Cassie halts, looking down the row, steps forward thinking, God, this is the end. God, please don't let Miriam …

She wavers by the closed curtain, feels a wave of nausea.

Good news about your friend, dear, a passing nurse says. It must be a relief.

Cassie startles. Good? She flicks back the curtain.

Casilda!

Now, now, Miriam, none of that silliness, Judith says, but smiles nonetheless.

Miriam's hair looks thin and lank, she's pale, more yellow than olive, but she is sitting up in bed, beckoning Cassie in with the arm not attached to the drip.

Cassie stands by the curtain and begins to cry.

Silly Silda, Miriam says quietly.

And Cassie moves forward, hugs her and laughs.

Sundown
March 1979

Judith will let me go back to college after the Passover holidays, Miriam says. I could have gone back at least two weeks ago, but you know how she fusses.

You were very ill, Cassie says.

Miriam's room is full of cards, several from The Gang, others from girls at sixth form after some persuasion from Cassie with the help of Joanne and Marcia. Today a large bouquet of peonies jostles amongst the cards.

From Tim, Miriam says, smiling.

Tim?

He's gone travelling — an adventure before Oxford.

Yes, he —

Broke up with Lorraine before he left. He came to see me.

He …

Don't look so shocked, Cassie, he's an intelligent person with taste. Why would he stay with someone like that?

So you and he are …?

Who knows? Perhaps. Miriam looks radiant. And chocolates as well. She points to a large purple box.

Don't you hate milk chocolate?

He doesn't know that, does he? He'll learn. Miriam grins. Now tell me everything that's happening at college.

Cassie knows that Miriam won't approve, but she mentions the concert anyway, wondering why she isn't more circumspect even as she tells her.

Please tell me you're not serious. It's not even music, just noise. And Sunderland, for goodness sake. Have I taught you nothing? Oh, God — unbearable — you are flying the nest only half-formed after all my efforts.

Miriam falls back on her pillows, dramatically.

I'm feeling rather queasy now.

Cassie laughs. She's really interesting, Miriam. Liam says it's all just squealing, but I've talked him into going.

Miriam scowls at the mention of Liam and Cassie wonders if she should have been more diplomatic, not have mentioned Liam.

It's called the Lionheart Tour. She's doing twenty-four concerts, Denmark and Germany and …

At least spare me the details, Cassie.

Miriam shrugs further into the bed.

I need to sleep now.

OK. I'll see you again soon.

There is no invitation to Miriam's house over the Easter holidays.

Cassie phones on Easter Monday, but Judith informs her that Miriam is out with a friend.

Who? Cassie blurts, wishing she'd thanked Judith and put the phone down.

Miriam has more going on in her life than you seem to think, Cassie, Judith says stiffly. Jayne is a friend from her opera group, actually, very talented young lady, very nice family, and of course they have a lot in common. Jayne doesn't go to Kate Bush concerts, for instance.

It might be the most Judith has ever said to her in one go, Cassie thinks.

Oh, she murmurs, thinking how pathetic she sounds.

But she phones the next day. The phone trills. When there is no answer she tries again, and again twenty minutes later, and again, so that she begins to hear the shrill dring of the phone when she's sitting alone in her bedroom wondering what to do with the empty afternoon.

She puts on *The Kick Inside* at high volume.

Turn that bloody racket down, her mother shouts within seconds.

Cassie sits on the floor next to her bed, listens to the first side of the album played quietly enough for her mother not to register 'the noise', turns it to the second side, moves on to *Lionheart*, singing along to 'Wow', which is in the charts.

She smiles to herself, thinking she's never had a clue about anything in the top ten before. When the album finishes she puts it on again.

She hears the phone ring, the tring in the hallway and no longer in her head.

Cassie!

She bounds downstairs, takes the receiver from her mother.

Hi, she says brightly. I called you earlier, but …

What do you mean? You couldn't call me earlier, I was at work, Liam says.

Oh, it's you, I thought …

Thanks! I was going to take you out for dinner tonight. Fancied a mixed grill at the *Red Lion*.

Sorry, I … Sorry, just been a bit of a weird day. That would be lovely. Really.

Yeah, better night out than that concert you're dragging me to anyway. You still sure you want to go?

Of course I am. April 12th. I'm counting the days. You might even enjoy it.

Doubt that very much. Can't make out a word she's screeching.

Wow, Cassie says.

What?

One of them is called 'Wow' — you hear the word over and over, unmistakable.

Don't be clever, Cassie, you know what I mean.

I still want to go. What time shall we meet tonight?

Cassie makes her way to the tutor group room on the first day of their last term.

Miriam is seated in the second row at a desk with Marcia Charles. There's a space at the desk in front beside Joanne Leigh, where Marcia normally sits.

I thought we could do with a change, Miriam says brightly, as though reading Cassie's thoughts. I always sit with Marcia in French and we share a dislike for a certain Liam Brennan after he disrupted that funeral so rudely. And apparently you and Joanne are both fans of the screaming Miss Bush.

Joanne smiles faintly, her face reddening to match the flame of her wiry hair.

I thought we could keep this convivial arrangement for history lessons too, Miriam adds, grinning. Judith is always telling me I need more friends. Practice for university too.

She turns her back on Cassie and whispers something in Marcia's ear.

A Tree Too Weak to Stand
November 1992

What really happened was that I was slow to learn. Belief wasn't so much my gift as my curse.

Cassie waits in the green room, another TV interview. She hopes that this time Liam won't be waiting outside for her.

She clasps a copy of the book, gazes at the cover: *This is the End of the Story,* a novel by Catherine Anne McManus. She will never again be Casilda. No more Cassie. No more Kitty Brennan.

All right, Titch? The boy at school had asked her.

Kat, she corrected. My name's Kat.

Why would anyone want to be called after a smelly animal? her mother asked. Your name's Cassie. Good enough for my mother and her mother before her. Too good for that sister of mine, but that's another story … Anyway, no-one's calling a child of mine Kat. What would people think?

Cats don't smell. They clean themselves. And …

That's enough lip. It's Cassie. Your name's Cassie.

Well, actually it's —

What did I just tell you?

Kat, she hisses under her breath.

Casilda, Miriam had insisted.

No, it's short for Catherine. It's a family thing …

Miriam shook her head. Catherine Anne McManus is only what you seem to be — it's an enchantment. You are Casilda of the Rising Moon. Have you read the book? Once there was a Moorish princess, Casilda …

There was an incident so slight, so small, so brutal that she could not go on.

She's just not what she seems …

Yes, Miriam had agreed. Yes.

The story and the facts no longer matched.

But Liam was there in front of her, holding her …

It's not a very pretty name, Liam told her the morning after their wedding. I mean, it does sound a bit short-tongued, like it should be Cathy, but I've never liked Cathy either.

I suppose I've got used to it. I tried being Kat when I

was little, but no-one ever called me that. Well, a couple of school friends did for a while, but it didn't stick. And Miriam —

God! Don't start on about Miriam …

Anyway, it's always been Cassie.

And you wanted to be called Kat? Really? Bit blunt. You need something … something more … Kitty. He said it like it was a revelation. Kitty, that's it.

What?

Your name.

I've never been … I mean I'm … It doesn't sound like me.

The all-new you. I love it. Liam and Kitty Brennan. Now that works. Yes?

I'm not …

Don't be negative, Cassie. You're always so — He stopped, laughed. I mean don't be so negative, Kitty. That's much better. You'll like it; you'll grow into it.

What really happened was that I told him I'd made a mistake. We'd only been married for a couple of months. I hated being called Kitty, but I didn't object for long. Then there was the night when I said I wanted to leave.

There was an incident so slight, so small, so brutal that she could not go on.

Liam held her down in the bed by the throat and told her

not to be stupid. But it wasn't true that she could not go on.

That year, she spent Boxing Day on a bench in the park, shivering in the snow, reading *Texts of Terror*, uncertain whether her tears were for Jephthah's daughter or herself. She thought about that beach, years ago, a man's hands around her throat.

Sometimes she told him again that she wanted to leave, but he told her she was being ridiculous …

There was a night when she sat on the bedroom floor shivering. Her clothes stuck to her, rain-sodden, icy. She couldn't remember how the argument had started or what it had been about; couldn't piece together why she'd left the house on a wet December evening, walked into the darkness; rain and wind harrying her. She waited to be told how ridiculous she was, began peeling off wet layers.

It's okay, Kitty, we can work this out. Have a bath, get some sleep. We'll talk. We'll talk properly. It's going to be okay, Kitty. We can do this. It's okay.

She poured hot water into the deep green bath, emptied in bath oil; all shall be well. In the hot bath she repeated — it's okay, Kitty, we can work this out. We can do this, she said aloud, sinking into jasmine bubbles.

She waited for him to start the conversation. How it would be okay, how years could be re-invented — narrative working backwards and forwards to make all things well.

She walked to the lake, sat on wall, watched clouds scudding over the hills, iced peaks reaching into the sky, remembered when the sky was simple; a light-blue crystal. She waited.

It was two weeks before she asked: This conversation — is it ever going to happen? Can we make it okay?

His look veered from surprise to disdain.

Ridiculous. No-one but you would take that seriously. Fucking hell, Kitty, what was I supposed to say?

She had been hysterical, running out into the rain, into the night, surely she must have realised he was only trying to calm her down.

I said what you wanted to hear, anyone would; the state you were in. Anyway, you don't want to talk. Not really. You never wanted to give it a chance.

It had been a blue November day two years ago when she again walked to the lake near her little cottage, sat on the wall to watch clouds scudding over the Moelwyns, iced peaks reaching high; remembered when the sky was simple.

When she returned home the house would be empty. But first she had walked to the post office, stopping at the bakery café to drink cappuccino.

No Liam today? The post office manager wore a red tie over his blue shirt, a thick watch with a broad leather strap.

He left, she'd said, smiling.

Oh. He nodded. It's Kitty, isn't it?

Catherine, she said. Catherine McManus.

In Turin, Catherine had sat at the dining table in the small room. Across the balcony a ring of high-rise flats surrounded a courtyard, the Alps beyond.

These are good, Fabio, personal, quirky, great evocation of place.

And my city? What do you think of my city?

It's beautiful, what I've seen of it so far.

He went to the kitchen, returned with two glasses, an open bottle of dark red wine.

So you will take my little book?

Yes.

Fabio smiled, sipped his wine. You went to the museum today?

Yes. You were right. An amazing building.

The Mole Antonelliana. It is the symbol of my city.

It was a synagogue?

It was meant to be. Antonelli was hired by the Jewish community, but kept changing the design, raising the cost. In the end the Jews pulled out, twelve years after building started. The city took over the Mole and the Jews had a new synagogue — in the Moorish style. Very beautiful. There were many like it in Europe, in Germany — destroyed on Kristallnacht.

I had a close friend who was Jewish, Catherine offered.

Ah. Fabio nodded. They have had a difficult time, he

ventured.

I've been writing about her. She's in the novel I have out in the autumn … a version of her, anyway …

Fabio nodded again.

She picked up his manuscript, flicking through it again. I love this passage where you talk about how we don't notice the best moments of our life until afterwards.

The next day, in Nice, she'd had time to visit the Chagall museum before a meeting with another author. She sat in front of 'Moses with the Burning Bush', felt herself falling:

… numinous burning, red and yellow against blue-blue-blue. Moses on his knees, transfigured — and I am transformed with him — the power of being: I will be who I will be. Raw energy. To be, to be new, to go on being, not to expire — to have a future — burning, always, not consumed. I was. I am. I will be. Will I?

She'd brushed away a stray tear, moved on to 'Noah's Ark':

… blue-blue waters rising, a bird here, goat there. And the people, waiting in the wings of apocalypse, huddled. Who will make it? There are mothers holding children, families clustered, a man on his knees, behind him a woman stands, head bent to his, arms wrapping him. Will they make it?

How many can an Ark hold? And the covenant, what is that? The rainbow promise of no more destruction? No one can make that promise, not even God, she thought, remembering a time when she believed, a time before she lost the baby, that savage flow of blood.

Again and again, the earth is wiped out. Tribulation. A people who are persecuted, and now? She tried to think of what Miriam would say about the images; whether the story and the facts would match.

... blue tribulation. Jacob meets the love of his life at the well and how does that go? Fourteen years before they are together. And his beloved child, his son — all that love come to tears, blood, betrayal, loss. And in the middle of this Jacob meets what? Who? Does he fight the ground of being for a place to stand? Jacob — violet on blue, struggling, fighting, changed —

Catherine conjured their first meeting — Your real name is ... It had taken her years to realise that Miriam had loved her. Yet, even Miriam had seen only the Cassie she had made up: Casilda. Catherine had believed all of it and none of it. And now? The Chagall haunted her:

... so we fight with being itself to discover who we are; limp on, walking out of a past of victories and defeats and into a future of unimagined losses, fears and hopes; wounded and blessed.

In the room of *Le Cantique des Cantiques* the canvasses were red.

Catherine had begun to weep, clutching her stomach.

Madame? The attendant reached out a hand tentatively, but pulled it back as Catherine looked up. *Madame? Vous ètes ...*

Catherine shook her head, stood. I'm fine. She'd brushed a hand ineffectually across her face, tried to smile. It's just the pictures ... they're very moving.

The attendant nodded, moved away, glancing back at her.

A knock on the door of the green room.

If you'd like to follow me, Dr McManus, they're ready for you.

Of course.

Catherine picks up her book, steadies herself for the interview.

Race Among the Ruins
March 1990

I didn't see Miriam for ten years. Afterwards I went home, went to bed, stayed there day after day, week after week, months lost in dreams or in memories I might have invented.

She waited for them to tell her she wasn't theirs. She took refuge under the table, cocooned from cigarette smoke fog, banter of television, fire flames spreading warmth only as far as the black leatherette sofa, where her mother's youngest brother jibed at her older sister. She hunkered beneath the folds of tablecloth, crouched into the fantasies they could not enter. Sometimes they passed food under the cloth.

Like a dog, the boy-uncle said, guffawing.

Kat, she hissed back. Kat.

At school she stood by the fence. A boy from the junior yard sauntered across, leant down, asked, are you okay?

She looked at him, puzzled.

I'm Ivan, he said. Are the other kids leaving you out?

I'm watching them. I'm making them up.

He looked at her, puzzled. You don't want to play?

I am playing, she told him. I'm playing 'they're my story'.

He shrugged. You shout me if they give you any trouble. All right, Titch?

Kat, she corrected. I'm called Kat.

Once she went to the sea. The sky was simple; a light-blue crystal. It may be fragile like me, she thought. She walked through marram grass, through dry cutting sand, red damp sand. The dunes hid a fat triangle of glass that pierced between her toes. Her mother, who hadn't yet revealed who she really belonged to, shooed her towards the first aid station. Her mother, who had lost her identity bracelet at the hospital after she had given birth and often joked that she couldn't be sure they'd given her the right baby, tutted and told her to go. She was not quite six years old. The flag of the station waved from the far end of the beach, almost as far as Marske, she thought, hobbling. The blood, redder than iron scars on wet beach, oozed, viscous. She felt strange; the sky sun-spattered, blue-vulnerable. Her imaginary friend, Marina, walked with her to the pole at the end of the stray. Nearly there, Marina said, encouraging her to hobble the last yards; foot throbbing, sand sticking to blood. Nearly at the place where the life-guard who doubled as first-aider wrenched the glass from between her toes, pressed hard to stop the blood, stuck plaster over the mess. She didn't know that she was allergic to sticking-plaster.

What took you so long? We've eaten the sandwiches. Her mother, who didn't believe in Marina, said, still not telling her that she wasn't theirs, lighting a cigarette, lying back against the dune.

She waited. Evening, and they were among the table legs and the adult's legs in Nanna's kitchen. It was raining and they couldn't go out to play. Not that she wanted to play her cousin's games; making mud pies, picking gooseberries, throwing a ball against a wall, kicking it. She felt draft as the door opened, heard the rustle of newspaper peeled off greasy parchment around fish and chips. Her cousins scuttered from the cover of table. She watched their legs, long grey socks sagging against plump calves; pictured their thick unwashed fingers digging into oily parcels; heard a hand slapped away.

Get off that fish, greedy little bastard.

The laughter of aunts, stench of oil, smoke, flesh.

A hand thrust a clump of chips under the table. She moved away.

Ignore them, Marina whispered, they're not your real family.

You should make her come out, an aunt-voice cackled, anyone would think we had a dog under there.

Kat, she breathed. Kat.

She peered out, watched her nanna, apron taut against the boulders of her chest, her old face a mask of expressions melting inside each other. Her nanna's hair, blue-black, backcombed, brittle. Her nanna's fingers, dead branches. She was looking for something in the large front pocket of her overall. She imagined a key, took it into her world, turned a lock in the crumb-strewn lino under the table, slipped away.

Memory, always made of objects; of good and bad smells,

or faded photos in a shabby scrapbook. There were three pictures of her as a baby. In all of them, black and white, edges peeling, she was crying from the depths of a Silver Cross pram, the behemoth model. She had had a replica for transporting her dolls, until her mother, who constantly said she didn't know who in the family the girl resembled, decided that 'almost-seven' was too old for dolls' prams and sent it to the tip. She closed her eyes and waited. No ideas but in things. Once she'd had two goldfish in the bowl. Then one. Her mother, who said perhaps she looked like the milkman or Whistling Rufus, who cleaned the windows that thickened with coal dust, told her she'd flushed one of the fish down the toilet in the yard.

They were fighting, her mother said.

Between the pram and the fish there was a dog. Patch rolled on the ground with her, listened to her stories. Her father, who seldom spoke, told her the dustbin lorry had frightened the dog away. Her mother, who constantly told her she didn't know where the girl got her ideas from, said Patch was smelly.

Good riddance.

She waited. They moved to a new house near the sea in Redcar. The sky, sulphur-coated, reeked of egg. The buzzers punched out the times of shifts: nights, days, earlies, lates. Flimsy houses on Wimpy crescents with rural names posed behind lawns dotted with rose bushes, marigold borders. The adults mocked the toddler next-door, blond head a beacon over spindle form, as he stumbled again and again.

Not very good on his pins, a neighbour bleated.

When the next-door family moved away, the little boy's leukaemia won.

The neighbours nodded; said sadly how they always knew there was something not right, poor little bugger.

Not right. She heard those words often. Not right. Always reading. Picks at her food. Too clever. At night she had nose-bleeds, fat drops of red ink inscribing her mother's best nylon sheets. Don't know where she gets it from, they'd whisper. When she slept, her ear, the one that couldn't hear, oozed black treacle onto the static-charged pillowcase. Not right.

She waited. They would tell her soon, she was sure.

Marina left long ago; she cannot remember exactly when, but now she has books and …

Casilda. It's who you really are — this is just an enchantment. Miriam had told her.

Who am I?

She wakes in the night, sits up in bed, asks the darkness, Who am I?

For God's sake, Kitty, go to sleep. Liam pulls the duvet tighter around his bulk.

No.

Kitty, it's three in the morning, we haven't all been in bed all day.

Go sleep somewhere else then.

What?

I don't want you in here. This is my room.

Fucking hell! Anything for a fucking bit of piece. There's no one as gifted as you at making a bad situation worse, is there?

Liam slams from the room.

She lies awake, drifts towards a half sleep.

The story and the facts must match.

Hands around her throat, rough breath, white cotton tearing, falling onto sand ...

She is by the sea. The sky is simple; a light-blue crystal. It may be fragile like me, she thinks.

The beach goes on forever, a boundary of coarse sand and marram grass further from the tide line, beyond that forestry, pine trees shading brown needles and stories of lost children. There is no one else walking here, a mile, two miles from the caravan site. They walk where the sand is wet, the shuck of bare feet on grains moist with salt and sea. Cassie watches the footprints, Miriam's slightly wider, longer. She is dressed in white, transparent cheesecloth floating from her thin torso on breaths of sea breeze, cotton skirt edged in lace.

She walks through marram grass, through dry cutting sand, red damp sand. The dunes hide a fat triangle of glass that pierces between her toes.

She sees Miriam on the beach, hurling a rock at the naked man who has her imprisoned in a sticky grasp ... feet on white sand, the rub of grains keening above the percussion of waves, Miriam circling away, the sudden halt ... There is a moment of sadness, opaque dark that drops and is gone, torn by the light. Miriam is transfigured: dazzling, serene; the beatific smile an instant before the unbearable moment —

On the beach he winds his arm around her as they walk, feeds her slices of chocolate orange.

They walk all the way to Marske, come off the beach near *The Ship Inn* ...

There is no one else on the beach. Only six footprints going on and on in the shoreline, his large, splayed. He wears blue swimming trunks ... His arm is around Cassie, his hand is sticky. Just do what I say ...

There is only smooth sand going on and on, but Miriam has a rock, jagged and dark.

No, Miriam says. No. She lifts both arms, hurls the rock, Cassie flinches away and the man looses his grasp, gasps, swears and they are running, towards the dry sand and marram grass, towards the forest, but Miriam is slower ... and he has her in his grasp, shaking her.

Run, Cassie, run!

Liam runs towards her from the beach as she rounds the last corner.

... hum rising to a howl, the sound that Cassie knows marks the margin between ecstasy and unconsciousness. She watches Miriam fall from his hold, watches him toe her roughly ...

She runs towards Miriam. God always demands sacrifice. Sand wails beneath feet. The rock in her hands, heavy, uneven. A Sunday school picture of Abraham about to sacrifice his son, because God had commanded it. Belief is your gift. The ram in the thicket.

... let justice roll down like waters, and righteousness like an ever-flowing stream. Did you bring to me sacrifices and offerings the forty years in the wilderness, O house of Israel?

... even Abraham didn't have to sacrifice his own son in the end, Miriam says to the tall curate. God provided an alternative.

She is the ram caught in the thicket on a beach in Nairn —

She sits on a bench shivering ... snow like white sand ... She reads *Texts of Terror*, uncertain whether her tears are for Jephthah's daughter or herself ... hands close around neck, ragged breath, white cotton tearing ... blood, redder than iron on wet beach, oozes, viscous. The sky sun-spattered ...

Nearly there, Miriam says.

Sand sticking to blood.

She falls onto sand ...

She's not what she seems ... another McManus slut ...

Yes, Miriam agrees, yes.

Yes ... hands around her throat, rough breath, white cotton tearing, blood welling between toes, red skin where the rock hits his thigh ...

Run, Cassie, run!

Liam runs towards her from the beach, holds her down by the throat, tells her not to be stupid ...

She wakes filmed in sour-milk sweat.

She sits up in bed, turns on the light, reaches for the journal that she hasn't written in for weeks. Writes:

Until death, it's all life, Cassie. Remember.

Yes, she says out loud to the night.

The unreason of the world is more insane than any fiction.

What really happened was that I didn't see Miriam for ten years.

Afterwards, I went home, went back to bed where I'd spent so much time since losing the child, slept day after day, week after week, until one March morning. I knew that I had to find her — Cassie, Kat, Casilda, Kitty … whoever she was, I had to find her.

Changes
September 1979

What really happened was that we became friends again when Miriam returned to sixth form after her spell in hospital; if 'friends' is the right word. We spent time together at The House, were otherwise polite and awkward, never mentioned Ben Haddaj or Casilda.

At college after A levels there was a fundraising weekend that leavers took part in; most joining in a beach run, some hiking near Roseberry Topping. Miriam decreed that we would do a sponsored reading of *The Lord of the Rings* and Miss Doone organised a rota of reluctant teachers to listen to us. No one else ventured into the room where we read on and on, twelve hours on Saturday, only four on Sunday, Miriam ending the torture with an episode from which she seemed to recover too quickly. It was the closest we'd been that year.

What really happened was this: the night before our marriage, I took my home-made Acrylic dress to Liam's mother's house in a carrier bag, so that we would wake up in different places on our wedding day.

In June, Liam gave Cassie an engagement ring, refashioned from one that had belonged to his grandmother. And her mother told her to leave home.

Bloody ridiculous, she hissed. All your chances and you're going to waste your life on that idiot. You're going to Cambridge, for Christ's sake. You could find a husband with money, and someone with brains, someone on your level. What's the use of an education if you won't use it?

You can't stay with us, Mandy said flatly. You'd hate it anyway. Me and Sean do nothing but fight. And he'd only pester you when he's drunk. Don't marry a bloody Brennan, Cassie, have some fucking sense.

Towards the end of July, Zoë announced a beach party with The Gang.

Mother of a blow out, Zoë said. Goodbye to all those going off to uni, our farewell before we leave for the barge, and an eighteenth bash for Cassie.

And to celebrate our wedding the next weekend, Liam added.

Sod that, Jeremy said, *sotto voce,* intending to be heard.

Thank you, Cassie interjected, so many changes.

She watched Miriam nestle closer to Tim, wondered whether Lorraine would come to the beach party.

Anyway, we'd better get going. We're not all skiving students. Liam shot a look towards Jeremy. Some of us have work to go to, he added. Come on, Cassie.

In the car back to the flimsy flat they shared in New Marske, Liam recited his litany of anxieties. How would he find a job in Cambridge? How could she think of leaving him only weeks after the wedding?

I won't need to leave you if you get a job there.

What job? Anyway, I'm earning good money here. I'd never get that anywhere else.

I thought people were leaving ICI for more pay.

On the rigs! You want me to go and work on the rigs now?

I didn't say that, I just meant … oh, nothing.

Don't go to Cambridge, Cassie. How are you going to fit in there anyway?

Miriam says …

Oh, fucking hell, don't start on about her.

They drove in silence. Slept facing away from each other, hugging the edges of the bed.

I thought we might give it a miss, Liam said, the morning of the beach party.

I'm going.

He ran water into the kettle. I'll take my guitar, he said, but Wearisome isn't touching it.

Lorraine was waiting for them as The Gang sauntered onto the beach. Miriam glanced at her, turned and kissed Tim, long and hard.

Lorraine, I'm so glad you came. Zoë put an arm around her. You can help me set out these blankets. Liam, can you find some stones for the corners? Cassie, we'll put food on the big checked one, but don't go in the small basket; it's got your birthday present in it. Tim, how about some driftwood for a fire? Jeremy too.

The Gang bustled into action, Lorraine and Cassie helping Zoë to set out food while Miriam trailed after Tim and Jeremy.

When Alex had the fire going, potatoes roasting in foil among the flames, they sat in a circle on the patchwork of blankets and Zoë handed Cassie a gift, a metal dove, the shape cut from bronze and enamelled by Zoë in cobalt blue, one jade eye.

It's beautiful, thank you. She slipped the leather thong holding the dove over her head.

We can sing happy birthday with the cake later, Zoë said, grinning and flushed. But how about getting the guitars out now?

Jeremy lifted his ancient instrument from the blanket beside him. Liam carefully took his shiny Ovation from its hard case.

Swap? Jeremy quipped.

Fuck off, Wearisome, Liam returned, but smiled

They worked through a repertoire of 'Alice's Restaurant', 'Oliver's Army', 'All along the watchtower', 'Maggie's Farm' … the supplies of beer and cider dwindling so that Terry and Stevie went on a mission to buy more.

After the feast of baked potatoes, Zoë produced a cake

with a flourish and a raucous chorus of 'Happy Birthday' ensued.

More song, Jeremy demanded.

'Moving strangers', Alex suggested.

Yeah, like this lot could sing Kate Bush. Jeremy strummed and giggled.

Lorraine began to sob loudly.

Lorraine? Oh, pet … Zoë hugged her close.

That was our song, Lorraine wiped snot from her face and glared at Miriam.

Let's go for a walk, Tim suggested, pulling Miriam to her feet.

Sorry, Lorraine, Jeremy said.

She nodded, tears coming fast again.

I bloody love that girl, Terry said, voice maudlin, gazing after Miriam, who was out of earshot with Tim, further down the beach. I should have said something when I had the chance.

You never had a chance, Stevie replied. She made it pretty clear your Teesside poly degree didn't interest her, Broth.

Terry nodded sadly, walked over to Lorraine and Zoë and wrapped his arms round both of them, swaying.

Whoa there, way to bring the party down, man, Jeremy quipped, false cheer making his voice too loud. How about 'Pretzel Logic'?

What's the chords? Liam asked too eagerly.

Here. Jeremy played a few bars. Stopped.

Show me again.

While Liam struggled to replicate the chords Jeremy had showed him, Lorraine and Terry sank onto the blanket together, both crying softly and rocking one another.

Like this. Jeremy leant over, tried to place Liam's fingers in the right configuration.

Liam pushed him away. Fuck off, pufter.

Don't be so soft, man. Just relax your fingers. He tried again to arrange Liam's tensed hand. The noise as Liam jerked away was of twanging strings, a crack of sheering wood. Lorraine's tears ceased. Alex and Terry lunged towards Liam too late to stop his fist exploding into Jeremy's face, blood and mucous spraying the remains of potato skins and birthday cake.

Shit! Jeremy doubled over. Shit! He rammed towards Liam, but Alex, Terry and Stevie blocked, Frank hovering on the edge of the melee, pale and uncertain, Tim running back towards them, leaving Miriam to trot behind.

On the morning of the wedding, Liam phones to say the car won't start, but he thinks he and Chris can push it downhill, not to worry.

I wasn't worried till you phoned, Cassie tells him.

She has hardly slept in the strange bed at Maria's house and, in the fifteen minutes since she got up, Liam's mother has criticised her hair (couldn't you put it up instead of leaving it all over the place?), her dress (the only bride to keep a dress in a carrier bag) and her taste (but everyone likes fruitcake. You have to at least have a bite when we cut the cake).

Liam giggles down the phone-line.

Are you drunk?

Fucking hell, Cassie, of course not, we had a drop of Cointreau, that's all.

I've got to go. Your mam's calling. Just don't be late.

What really happened is this:

I find the gift in the porch of Liam's mother's house as we are setting out for the registry office. The note reads:

I can't come to your wedding. How can I? M.

Inside, a set of knives wrapped in tissue paper.

Never too Close
November 1990

This is what really happened. I saw Miriam again and it was another year before Liam left.

I went to bed, stayed there. But spring came and I decided to listen to Miriam — until death, it's all life.

I come to Toledo to seek her out — Casilda, Cassie, Kat, Kitty, Catherine ... I come to Toledo to find her and write. But Casilda is as elusive as reality. Ben Haddaj, if he ever existed, has fallen out of history, lives only in the pages of a worn children's paperback that I've carried with me. Toledo resonates to a Moorish past — the tiles on the walls, the dishes in the tabernas, the curved swords displayed in shops, the shape of keyhole archways, the Arabic designs on the intricate damascene jewellery of oxidised black steel inlaid with filigree silver and gold adorning every other shop window. Yet little of the eleventh century can be touched: stones in the wall perhaps; though not the Puerta Vieja de Bisgara, rebuilt over centuries; not the Alcazar, completely rebuilt.

In the tenth century cave that houses the Museo de la Espana Magica I step into a dwelling that existed when Casilda lived here; on the walls of the entrance, hands of

Fatima, one of them perfectly preserved, surrounded by three elegant dark birds. The hand of Fatima, the hamsa, the laminated museum card tells me, is a five-fingered symbol to ward off the evil eye and bring protection. In Jewish tradition it is known as the hand of Miriam, a symbol of the Torah and of the five senses with which to worship God, as well as a magical charm.

The hand of Miriam, I say out loud.

At the Church of Cristo de la Luz, the little square end of it once a mosque, Mezquita Bab al-Mardum, I come to a building Casilda might have seen, touched. Would a Muslim princess have ever left the Alcazar?

I circle the four stone columns, stand under horseshoe arches, move between the nine ceiling vaults gazing at their intricate designs. Have I been here before, looked up through cusped arches, contemplated the quibla wall?

The day is cool, bright. Is there a rustle of silk on skin or only air thickening in shadows beneath vaulted arches, screened from winter glare by panels of wooden lattice?

In the mosque gardens, trees bow under approaching winter, dry leaves shimmer, fall; the large cedar bends to the wind. There are none of the fruit trees I imagined here, no peach, apricot, guava or fig hunkering against the winter. The fountain by the back wall is empty, yet I turn towards a sound of water against stone. Is there a word in the breeze? *Tulaytula.*

I walk back uphill towards my apartment, narrow lanes, cobbles underfoot. Has the city forgotten Casilda?

Nights are cold, almost freezing. In the tiny apartment I delve into the intricately carved chest, mahogany grain, scent of cedar inside, pull out wool blankets patterned with orange arches, earthen curves, ochre spirals.

Between waking and sleeping, she enters my skin.

I turn in the night, watch Miriam sleep; olive skin, hair a tangle of soot and pitch. So many defeats ago, I think, you chose me. I thought I was the ram caught in the thicket, the replacement sacrifice. I used to warn you not to go looking for trouble and now ...

Miriam's breath catches and she turns in her sleep. Does she whisper something? I reach out, stroke Miriam's face. Her eyes open and she holds out her arms.

Remember, my darling Casilda. Remember, Miriam says, and if you can't remember, invent ...

Remember how you studied the *Qu'ran* from the age of five, how you heard the story of Saint Marina, were fascinated by a king's daughter who ran away to lead a contemplative's life. You learned with the wisest in the taifa, became brilliant, but remained restless, disturbed by the thought of prisoners in the palace dungeons until you took them food, heard their stories, remembered Saint Marina.

What are you carrying, princess?

The soldier blocks my passage down the steps. I shrink inside the hooded cloak, colour of night sky, lift folds of a white silk robe closer, the loaves hidden.

Roses, I say.

I feel the tremor, darkness falls on me before I've hit the

ground. When I come round, the steps beneath are strewn red, the air thick with the scent of roses.

At Mezquita Bab al-Mardum the next day, air cooler, sky brighter, azure almost white, there is a rustle of silk, shadows congeal beneath vaulted arches. In the garden water bells against stone, whispers, *Casilda*.

A heavy clot of blood slips between my legs. Unsteady, I glance round. No-one. I huddle into my cardigan, wrap my coat around my body to hide the blood I feel oozing through layers of clothing, begin the climb back to the apartment through steep narrow streets, cobbles jarring, abdomen aching.

Miriam walks beside me.

Casilda fell sick, she says. Remember. It was the same illness that your mother died from not long after your birth. There was no way to stop the blood.

I hunch into the pain, feel stickiness seep through thick wool tights. A spasm halts me.

One of the prisoners told you about the wells of Saint Vincent near Briviesca in la Bureba. And so you persuaded your father to send you there to be healed, became an ascetic like Saint Marina.

I begin the slow trudge again. I can see the studded wooden door set in rough stone that lets onto the courtyard where my apartment shelters.

Remember the night of your death, how you sent your spirit across Spain to Toledo to be with your father as he passed away. Some stories say you lived to be over a hundred, but we know you died young. Perhaps neither of us stays in a body for long once we are parted from each other.

I push against the heavy slats of wood, slump onto the herringboned brick floor of the courtyard, waves of nausea throbbing through me, rise, inch towards the worn wooden steps up to my door, my hand clammy on the metal rail.

Inside, I stand on the cool cobalt tiles of the bathroom, let water scald and saturate every sense.

Blood strews the drain crimson, tang of iron on tongue, water seers, soothes.

A shadow pale as dust flits across a mote of light, the fragrance of roses suffusing the air. Somewhere a string is plucked, faint music —

> Al-'ūdu qud tarannam
> Bi-abdā'i talhīn
> Wa ŝaqqod al-madā nib
> Riyād al-basātîn

When I step out of the shower, the flow of blood has ceased.

Here, Miriam says, enfolding me in a white towel. And this, she adds. She holds out a white knitted shawl that I've never seen, but know from the pages of *Casilda of the Rising Moon*, pulls it around me. It's a cold night, she says, get under the blankets. I'll make you some mint tea.

I slide between white cotton sheets, drowse.

When I wake, the sky is dark, sharp stars through shutters. On the bedside table of dark wood, a silk cord of palest blue, strung with a tiny hand of Miriam in damascene. Beside it a turquoise glass of mint tea has cooled.

Did She Mention My Name?
September 1989

I hadn't seen Miriam for ten years.

Trust me, Cassie, you'll get your island.

My island became a recurring dream, an island no one had ever stepped on, but there it was … An island I could not escape so instead I slept through days and nights, oblivion my only comfort.

Hello? Could I speak to Cassie Mc, I mean Brennan, Cassie Brennan, please.

Catherine. I mean, yes — speaking.

Cassie? It's Judith.

Catherine pauses. Judith?

Miriam is death speaking.

I will never leave this room, she says, voice thinner than the light edging round the curtains.

The room smells of night-sweats, sweet decay, oranges.

So tell me about your life, she instructs before I have even said hello, asked hollow questions about how she is.

I sit beside her. Oranges, I say. Miss Doone wouldn't approve.

There is a ghost of smile. Girls, there are only two rules here, she says, her voice precisely aping our memory of Miss Doone, always walk on the right and never bring oranges to school.

I laugh, blot out the exhaustion that has greyed Miriam's face.

She had migraines, you know. Oranges were her trigger — though I didn't find that out for years.

If she'd told us that Penny Dean would have brought them in deliberately, she whispers.

Perhaps, I say.

We fall silent, both begin to say something at the same moment, trail away. I shift in my seat, feel the odour of dying lilies cling to my pores.

And how's Tim?

Didn't work out.

She turns her head away so that lank black hair falls over her face.

Oh, I'm sorry, I …

Still blissful on your island with Liam I suppose, she says

into the pillow.

Well … actually we've … I mean …

I can taste oranges clotting my throat.

Do you remember when Miss Doone thought …

No, she says. No, I hardly remember anything now.

Silence gnaws into the afternoon.

You'll come again?

Judith has aged more than ten years, I think.

She really asked for me?

She asked for Casilda. One of those silly games you played as children. There is a flicker of the Judith I once knew as she speaks, then she sags again.

She's determined to die, Cas … Catherine.

She can't just decide to die. Was it a terrible episode?

The worst, but she recovered. Physically recovered. She ran away from the hospital in her nightdress. She was …

Judith puts a hand to her throat, swallows hard, holds herself stiff.

She was in the street … raving … about illness and dreaming …

In sickness I had such strange dreams, so strange I fear to tell you lest you think me insane, I supply for her.

Yes. Yes, that's it. You were very close, weren't you? I shouldn't have …

I put a hand on Judith's arm, the first time I've ever touched her, I think.

She shakes herself slightly.

They would have committed her, Cas — I'm sorry — I know it's Catherine now.

It doesn't matter.

A thin smile.

They wanted to lock her away, but her neurologist was very good. So here she is, determined to die. You will come again?

Yes.

Thank you, Catherine.

Who are you? Miriam asks when I return.

Miriam! You know who it is. Judith shakes, tries to hold herself still. You have to stop this, Miriam, you …

She leaves the room and I hear her begin to sob on the landing.

It's Cassie, I say, wondering if I should go after Judith.

I'm sorry, I don't know anyone of that name, Miriam says.

Casilda, I say. It's Casilda.

No, I've never known a Casilda. I've been ill. I'm confused by ghosts. Perhaps I knew you, I don't remember.

Once you found a girl and called her Casilda, I continue her.

I don't remember, she says again, voice brittle.

Miriam!

I see the trace of a shudder. There is a moment of sadness, opaque dark that drops and is gone. Miriam is transfigured: dazzling, serene; the beatific smile an instant before the unbearable — the uneven jerk of her limbs, the hum rising to a howl, the sound that marks the margin between ecstasy and unconsciousness, the stare signalling her absence.

Judith is in the room before I can call her name.

Oh, Cassie, she's …

No. No, she's unconscious. She's …

Judith leans over, begins to search for pulse, breath, shaking as she works.

The grey September afternoon falls away and there is only the story that Miriam told me; belief is my gift for one aching second before the room swims back into consciousness, Judith howling beside her daughter's body.

God, this is the end of the story. I can't go on, I whisper to no one.

Fine as Fine Can Be
June 1994

Catherine tries to remember his directions, but soon she is lost in a maze of narrow mediaeval streets. She tracks back downhill, returns to the square beside the basilica. The sun is hot, the streets empty. She crouches by a wooden door. Breathes deeply. Begins to walk uphill. She carries the image of the apartment with her — its white bedspread and green shutters; its stone wall and the niche where she placed the citrus candle; its weathered desk and two armchairs; scents of lemon and salt, linen and love-making. She comes to a fork, two paths leading upwards. She considers, notices a gap in the wall to the left. There it is, the famous Menton cemetery, the one he'd returned from red-faced, perspiring, but triumphant; a new story ready to fill another notebook, new photographs to show her.

She tracks slowly through the tiers of tombs and mausolea, the cosmopolitan dead shaded from the glare of the sun. Half way up the necropolis she encounters a couple. They stand with mouths half open, hands tightened around the iron bars of a monument, among wreaths of flowers, in the thick grey of all those bodies and under a low heavy sky. The woman pants heavily; a too-tight top streaked with sweat, fanning her face with her hat. He smiles — a thin smile, so much effort.

Hot, he manages to say.

The woman stares at her, snorts in the direction of the man, heads uphill.

She climbs upwards on another path, finds a deep balcony overlooking blue ocean, blue sky, remembers the first day in the room when they opened the shutter that looks across the old town, out to sea.

They'd met for the second time at the tail-end of 1992, after she'd taken on his manuscript. They sat for hours in a café like earnest teenagers, swapping opinions on Béla Tarr's *Werckmeister Harmonies*, Bruno Schulz's *Street of Crocodiles*, the poetry of C D Wright, the jazz of Oliver Nelson; *More Blues and the Abstract Truth*. At their first editorial meeting in the museum in Birmingham they discussed the language of Beckett and Joyce, the untrustworthiness of petty politicians. When they lunched together a fortnight later they'd raved about the short stories of Jesse Ball, the beauty of *Tree of Codes*. They talked for three hours, neither of them raising the question of what they might be starting to mean to one another.

Yet they had navigated here, together, last summer. On their last evening in Menton they'd walked along the sea wall, looked out at the picture-book dazzle of moonlight on water, how it spread from the luminous centre to the margins of the dark; his words, the waves, shushing her tears.

Across the cemetery the couple heave up a slope. She hears the woman telling the man he'll burn, as though talking to a recalcitrant child. She looks away, gazes out across the blue bay. When she turns again, the woman is taking wipes from her bag, dabbing at the man's face, adjusting his sunglasses.

She smiles, heads downhill. My headache has gone, she

thinks. She will go back to the empty apartment, begin the next round of editing Fabio's manuscript before their meeting in Turin.

She stops for coffee at Bar du Cap, evening stealing the light of the orange afternoon bit by bit as she sips, but the heat remains even as the sun sinks. On their first full day in Menton last year, it had rained, she remembers. She needs a distraction to stop herself from dwelling on his absence. The room will be an empty shell, she thinks, walking towards the sea rather than heading back to the narrow street beneath the basilica, the sound of bells, the incline of cobbles. Beneath the Bastion the water is like glass moving around rock.

She forces herself back to the apartment.

She sits at the desk and begins reading Fabio's novel.

She fingers the picture of Simon propped on the desk. Smiles.

On their first day in the apartment last summer they had stood together in the little living room, bodies pressed together, trembling.

The night before he left Menton on that first trip, she had cried so many tears she had feared the ocean would overflow. He held her, soothed her *his words, the waves, shushing her tears.*

When she's alone she still wonders if — after all — she has made him up, but no — he is waiting for her at home, and last autumn they had lived through a strange month, apart and then together in Budapest, while she researched the novel she is writing now. She has not invented him — they talk across the miles each evening; spooling in distance, standing beneath the same moon, planning …

She cannot stop the memories, much fingered as they are.

In the white-walled flat there is only silence. Across the sea a moonbeam path.

Alone, she drifts in almost-sleep, slips through a mirror into another world:

Sun turns to snow, night to day, sea to land. In this bleached-grey place of dream, she is lost. I too am lost, she thinks she hears him say. She steps through another mirror in search of him, a splinter of glass piercing her heart. She has carried his heart through the glass.

The room swells, slips back, swells forward again. She lies back on the bed, sheets crisp and cool.

In the dream, Liam tells her to walk to find her lover, thousands of miles, knows she will fail. But another voice murmurs, belief is your gift. In the looking glass world are many mirrors. She steps through another, longing for him, a fragment of glass splitting her tongue, one drop of blood falling onto sand. She has carried his name through the glass.

She moves among mirrors lined up in rows along the shore, some have dust covers, some glare, brazen-faced; each frame distinct: thin strips of pine; ornate gilt, chipped or pristine, cherubbed or rose-encrusted; silver swirls; polished mahogany. Among silvered faces, some are Sunday-school scrubbed, others pitted, smeared, dulled.

I'm still here, she says to the faces of glass; *I'm still here.*

Vous m'avez reconnue
Je suis la meme
Et pourtant autre

She walks between the mirrors, aisle after aisle, the beach expanding with each step. She paces faster, past mirrors that dazzle, leer, some illuminated, others distorted; she strides past images, their voices luring, hissing, coaxing, scoffing; runs between aisles that narrow and stretch for miles; darts faster, tripping, reaching out a balancing hand that brushes a slender glass that totters, rocks, settles only after it has grazed the next, which quivers, sways, pitches forward into the next, the next the next the next the next, glass shattering in a banshee cacophony, shards clinking, wailing, wood cracking, exploding, metal clanging, a million echoes jingling, air reverberating devastation before diminishing to chiming, chinking, tinkling, before waning to silence, bristling.

She stands still. A fragment of glass spears between her toes, blood pooling onto white sand.

She has toppled all the mirrors to find this one, so that — stepping through she will be with him again. She walks through glass, leaves the broken pieces behind. There is no blood. *I'm still here*, she tells him.

Catherine wakes, sheets wound round her, rumpled.

She sits up, puts a hand on her warm belly, the bulge ripening, says to the morning, This isn't the end of the story.

Acknowledgements:

The seed of this book germinated many years ago and grew slowly. Many people have shared its journey — thank you to each of you. Particular thanks to the writing groups who have attended courses I've taught at Ty'n y coed and listened to early drafts; to my family for their continual support and to Adam Craig, not only for his valuable feedback, but also for taking me to Toledo to complete the novel.

Quotations from and allusions to *Don Quixote* by Miguel de Cervantes are from the Gutenberg Project edition, translated by John Ormsby.

The quote '...to write, something has to go adrift in life, we have to no longer be able to take reality for granted.' is from Simone de Beauvoir, *The Prime of Life*, Marlowe & Co, 1st Paragon Edition.

The poem fragment:

Al-'ūdu qud tarannam
Bi-abdā'i talhīn
Wa ŝaqqod al-madā nib
Riyād al-basātîn

['The lute began to resound with the most beautiful melodies, and the brooks flowed gaily through the flower gardens.'] is from *Hispano-Arabic Poetry; an Anthology*, translated by James T Monroe, Gorgias Press.

The quotation from Amos 5:24-25 is from the New Revised Standard Version Bible, copyright © 1989 the Division of

Christian Education of the National Council of the Churches of Christ in the United States of America. Used by permission.

Allusions to Dostoevsky on the subject of epilepsy are taken from *The Unpublished Dostoevsky: Diaries & Notebooks 1860-81* (Vol. 3), Fyodor Dostoyevsky, translated by Arline Boyer, First Thus Edition, 1976.

There are several websites in English and Spanish with competing but sketchy accounts of the life of Casilda. I have taken my inspiration from several sources and added my own interpretations, but am grateful to Elizabeth Borton de Trevino's children's novel, *Casilda of the Rising Moon*, Penguin, 1967, which I first read in 1972.

The titles of the chapters are taken from song titles by the Canadian folk singer, Gordon Lightfoot.